A Love Like Ours

A Love Like Ours

Rebecca Karadağ

Published in 2020

Cover photograph: unknown source

First printing: 2020

ISBN: 9798662626331

For you my love, no distance could ever be too far.

And for my mother, who always believes in a little magic.

"I already love in your beauty, but I am only beginning to love in you that which is eternal and ever precious – your heart, your soul. Beauty one could get to know and fall in love with in one hour and cease to love it as speedily; but the soul one must learn to know. Believe me, nothing on earth is given without labour, even love, the most beautiful and natural of feelings."

COUNT LEO TOLSTOY

Chapter One

I'd wanted to come here my whole life. The song echoed in the streets below. It was magical – the call to prayer. It may have only been five in the morning but I was spellbound. The sun rose, an orange hue lighting the city. Another foreign land awaited me, one I'd always dreamed of.

I must have dozed off a little. I'd had hardly any sleep – bloody airport delays. I'd waited three hours in a stuffy airport and ran into a rather unpleasant security guard at customs. The spices weren't perhaps the best idea but I wasn't smuggling drugs that's for sure. He'd interrogated me for close to three quarters of an hour, he loved every minute, and I just about made the flight. I'd munched through half a bag of crisps with a screaming toddler at my side – not mine either I may add. None of that now mattered, I was here. My phone vibrated and I squinted at the screen. It was my mother. I'd hardly managed a hello.

'Hello beautiful' she beamed.

Her voice reminded me of home and I couldn't help but smile at that very thought. She had always been such a pure soul, her infectious smile bringing nothing but love. That aside, she was stunning. Her ash blonde curls ran effortlessly down her back, her skin flawless.

'How're you sweetheart? How was the flight? What's the hotel like?' she asked, her questions endless.

'I'm fabulous' I said with a hint of sarcasm.

'It's going to be wonderful darling, I just know it. And, you never know, you may just meet Mr. Tall, Dark and Handsome after all.'

She'd always longed for me to find love and settle down – something which didn't seem likely anytime soon. Truth is, romance was the last thing on my mind.

'I'll keep you updated' I replied, humouring her.

'And Rose, next time take me with you' she said softly.

We'd holidayed together year after year, each trip as fabulous as the next but I needed to go this one alone. It was *the end of an era* as she had put it.

'I love you' I said sincerely.

'I love you to the top of the Eiffel Tower and back' she replied.

We had visited Paris when I was little and I fell in love with the city at first sight. She'd said this to me ever since.

I ended the call, feeling loved. Home would have to wait as I wasn't yet done with finding myself, as all travellers seem to say. I opened the wooden shutters, my senses instantly awakened. The smell of freshly baked bread from the streets and the strong scent of jasmine from the gardens below filled the air. The sound of traffic mirrored the view of the bustling city. I admired the aged, mosaic tiles, chipped and faded, amplifying the character which the city undeniably held. Istanbul, you had my heart already.

I was still in my nightie. I should probably get dressed. I'd never quite fit that typical tourist image, even though it would be more practical to do so. I'd spent most of my student loans building up the perfect wardrobe – Aspinal of London, Dolce & Gabbana, Manolo Blahnik. I'd become obsessed with designers from the get go. I'd keep copies of *Vogue* (every month from when I was about five – yes there were hundreds) in my room. Carrie Bradshaw was the inspiration. Mum would let me watch *Sex and the City* from an early age. I didn't get the references but Carrie's walk-in-wardrobe was the dream. Over time, I began to relate to it more and more. Carrie said *"It's hard to walk in a single woman's shoes. That's why we need really special ones now and then to make the walk a little more fun."* – And I couldn't agree more.

3

I picked a white broderie anglaise dress which flowed just past the knee, jewelled sandals and an ivory leather tote – very chic if I do say so myself. I checked the look one last time and stepped out into the hall. I was hungry. I hadn't eaten since those crisps on the flight and even they hadn't filled the void. The restaurant was bigger than I'd expected, filled with wooden tables adorned with white linen clothes and oil lanterns. The area extended onto a veranda for alfresco dining. I wished I'd come down a little earlier. I only had ten minutes at best. I poured myself a glass of orange juice, picked what looked like a pastry from the buffet and sat at a small round table in the corner.

'Coffee Madam?' asked a pristine waiter.

He held a chrome plated cafetière and a white linen serviette was placed across his arm. This hotel was fabulous. It was the last chapter of my travels so why not splash out a little. That's what went through my mind when I booked the place.

'No, thank you' I beamed in response.

I wasn't in the mood for coffee. He bowed his head and swiftly turned away.

I sipped the juice and placed a serviette in my lap, taking a bite of the layered pastry. I had always been favourable of fresh croissants yet this was different. Thin layers of flaky phyllo filled with spinach and feta cheese. I gulped the rest of the juice before brushing away the pastry crumbs. I cast a smile towards the waiter as I left and he bowed his head once more.

I made my way down to the foyer, picking up a business card before stepping outside. The heat hit me. I'd expected the summer months to be hot but I hadn't quite bargained for the humidity. I was about to step back into the air conditioning when a man approached me. He was middle aged, his greying beard aged him more so, and of average height. His build implied his love for all things sweet.

'*Günaydın*' he said.

I had no clue what he had said but luckily he switched to English.

'Good morning. Are you partaking in the tour of the old city today?' he said with a slight accent.

I was a little surprised at his proficiency of English but then again he was a tour guide. I'd love to get lost in another language I thought.

'Yes, I'm Rose' I replied.

He proceeded to cross my name of his list. 'It is a pleasure to meet you Rose. My name is Mustafa. Shall we?' he posed, gesturing towards the group stood at the end of the street.

The group sported ugly shorts and backpacks. I didn't fit that typical tourist label after all. Mustafa marched forward with a multi-coloured umbrella at his side. We followed his every move through the cobbled streets. The buildings either side of us were tall enough so that nothing was to be seen beyond them. Mustafa lead us into what I would consider to be the heart of the city. Tram lines painted the city floors whilst street food vendors lined them.

The smell of grilled meats, herbs and spices would satisfy any traveller. Gardens and fountains lay beyond these streets, bringing a different tone into the picture. Oil lanterns lined the greenery, lighting even the day. I was in awe.

Mustafa raised his arms and loudly spoke the word *Hoşgeldiniz*. That one foreign word, unbeknown to me, rolled off his tongue.

'Welcome to Sultanahmet, the historical heart of the city. 1603 was the year...' he began.

I listened, intrigued. The wisdom he held was mirrored in his eyes – tones of hazelnut and amber in the iris swirled into darkness.

Words echoed through the city. I glanced up, a dome visible beyond the trees.

'*Ezan*, the Islamic call to prayer' stated Mustafa. 'It is now time to explore The Blue Mosque. Follow me' he ordered and that's exactly what we did.

'Wow' I whispered.

The beauty which stood in front of us was truly magnificent. I closed my eyes, swallowing the song.

'It is fairly remarkable, is it not?' asked Mustafa.

My mouth ajar, I couldn't seem to reply but my head nodded in agreement.

He chuckled. 'She has this affect on many.'

The queue was a mile long. I was renowned for being impatient and blamed the London lifestyle for that. Hundreds of people rushed around the city to get to their ordinary jobs in their ordinary lives. Here, people seemed carefree, they seemed happy.

It was almost midday. The sun was beating down and the shade nonexistent. I was fair-haired and unfortunate enough to be blessed with the palest skin. I was envious of the olive complexions surrounding me. Dark ringlets and golden undertones – that was the dream. I rummaged in my tote for the factor fifty and began applying it to my shoulders.

'Madam' said Mustafa in a hushed tone.

I looked his way. The group glared at me.

'I do not wish to speak out of terms but in Islam it is considered respectful to cover one's shoulders. Perhaps you have a shawl?' He glanced disapproving at my bare skin.

I'd spent weeks in The Middle East but the thought to bring a scarf today had slipped my mind. I looked at him blankly. I felt foolish as the others gawked my way. It is funny isn't it? People seem to stare at you more when you're travelling alone.

'This is no problem Madam. If you would permit me to suggest the purchasing of a garment from one of the nearby sellers' he said, gesturing towards the line of market stalls to the left of us.

I don't know whether it was his accent but he seemed to have such a way with words. It was like getting lost in the pages of a classic novel. I smiled and walked towards the market sellers. I was thankful to leave the queue, even if it was for a moment. It was moving far too slowly for my liking. I made my way towards a stall draped in cloth and a woman greeted me.

'*Hoşgeldin canım*' she said as she motioned towards her goods.

I seemed to recall that was the same word Mustafa had spoken yet I didn't trust my nonexistent Turkish so I just did what any traveller would do and smiled. I cast my eyes across the array of cloth lining the stall, brushing my fingers along the fabric. Vivid, yellow silks, embroidered cotton and elaborate patterned stitching. I dilly-dallied for quite some time before deciding on an orange, cotton shawl with white embroidery along the edges. It was beautiful – unlike anything you would find in a high-street store. The woman smiled as I handed it to her. She threw it across my shoulders, approving of my choice. I reached inside my tote for my purse as she pinned something onto the fabric. I looked down to see a safety pin now accessorising the garment. The bead was painted with a blue eye. I wasn't sure of the meaning but it was pretty enough. She held her hand out for payment.

'How much?' I asked.

She frowned. It was no surprise that she didn't speak English. She pointed to a white tag, the number seventy handwritten upon it. This was a bargain but I guess there was no designer label to triple the price. I handed the notes across and she threw the money to the floor. She then picked it up again, smiling as she bowed her head in gratitude. I disregarded it as some kind of custom as she seemed happy enough with her sale. I thanked her, as best I could, and headed back to join the group.

I didn't recognise anyone. And then I saw something in the distance – a multi-coloured umbrella. The group were now almost at the entrance. Don't you just love that? I had a skip in my step as I joined them once more.

'You made the right choice' Mustafa stated, admiring my purchase.

'Thanks' I replied, blushing slightly.

'*Teşekkür ederim*' he said.

I guessed this was how you said thank you in Turkish as he didn't explain himself. I repeated the word several times under my breath.

He smiled and said '*Sağol* will be fine' – obviously I hadn't quite mastered it.

I'd always try to converse in the native tongue yet I'd never come across Turkish or, for that matter, Turks before. Many didn't bother. I mean, why would you? *Everyone speaks English anyway.* I shook my head at the small minded comment which I had heard more than once, attempting to master the pronunciation.

'And I see that you wear the *nazar boncuğu*' he added.

'Pardon?' I asked, looking at him blankly.

'The bead you wear. The blue eye is an amulet thought to protect against evil. That's if you believe in that sort of thing' he said, searching my face.

'Well...' I mumbled.

9

Truth be told, I wasn't even sure myself if I believed in superstitions. I think he saw this in my eyes.

The entrance to the mosque was magnificent. A large wooden door, lined with guards, awaited us.

'Please remove your footwear and women ensure that your head, shoulders and knees are covered' he informed.

Thankful that my dress was just beyond knee length, I slipped off my sandals, placing them neatly to one side. I pulled the shawl over my head, allowing the material to drape across my shoulders. The cloth shaded my hair and skin from the burning sun. I waited behind Mustafa as the rest of our group scampered to remove their trainers.

'Please be respectful. This is our place of worship' reminded Mustafa. 'Shall we enter?' he posed and we nodded our heads in unison.

Exquisite – the only word to describe it. A royal blue carpet painted the floor, holding mats which I assumed to be used for prayer. The walls were intricately painted and tiled, boasting countless patterns teamed with gold leaf writing. The domed ceiling brought a sense of greatness from which candles and lanterns hung to the floor, lighting the darkness. Arched windows permitted rays of light to enter from all angles. The beauty and grandeur of this place entwined to create something spectacular.

'You were wowed before, so what are you now?' Mustafa whispered in my ear, smugness in his voice.

Words failed me as I turned to him, only able to cast a smile.

There were many still praying. I can't say that I had ever been very religious myself. Religion seems to be the root of all evil in this world and I couldn't help but wonder why. I'd visited many countries these past few months. And in spite of culture, religion and language, I'd since come to realise that it is love which remains a constant.

We were soon ushered towards the exit. No amount of time would be enough to appreciate the detail this place had to offer. The sun was blinding. I rummaged inside my tote to find my sunglasses – Chanel – a gift from an old flame. I couldn't think of him, not now. I gazed up towards the sky, birds flying low overhead.

'Rose?' said Mustafa.

I came back down to earth. 'Sorry. I was just...' I began.

'Admiring the beauty' he said, reading my mind.

Beyond the wisdom, the love he had for his country was apparent. I smiled as I slipped on my sandals.

'I now permit you a short break. Please use this time wisely' said Mustafa.

The rest of the party posed in front of the mosque. I spied a bench in the distance. I sat and inhaled deeply, shaded by the trees and pretty pink blossom. It's so easy to lose sight of what lies in front of you. I looked upon the perfect postcard view. Minutes passed as I let my thoughts run wild. I was not yet ready to return to the life I'd left behind, to the ordinary life I had led. I needed something more. I wanted something more than just ordinary. A little magic would do. I heard Mustafa's voice in the distance signalling that the break was over. He spoke of famous Sultans and historic wars. The past was fascinating but what of the future. Who knows for how long we will be here. The names he rattled off had accomplished so much in their lifetimes. I'd be lying if I said I hadn't achieved anything but right now I felt like I was stuck in limbo. I was living a life between the reality and the dream. And for the life of me I didn't even know what the dream was.

'Shall we?' Mustafa called and marched forward.

We weaved in and out of narrow, cobbled side streets. High buildings with shuttered windows and wooden balconies lay either side. Each street looked the same as the next. We travelled deeper into a maze. It was cooler here. Many locals sat outside their homes, watching the world go by. Mustafa walked by my side. His aroma was one of tobacco combined with lemon zest. I pictured him sat in an armchair sharing his wisdom with countless grandchildren as his wife baked goods for them all to enjoy. We turned down yet another street and came to an archway. Woven rugs hung at the entrance. The word *Kapalıçarşı* welcomed us.

'The Grand Bazaar, one of the largest and oldest markets in the world' Mustafa said with pride. 'Over 4, 000 shops spread over 60 streets await us.'

Now this was my kind of tour. I'd always found that any mood could be instantly lifted with the purchase of something pretty which you didn't necessarily need. I had hoped to find some hidden gems upon this trip.

'I cannot however guide you through the bazaar as space will not permit a large group to do so. I will wait here for your return. The merchants in this city are honest but, on occasion, some will be inclined to rip you off so be sure to haggle before agreeing to their initial price. One could spend days in the bazaar but you have ninety minutes. You will find me indulging in coffee and baklava here if you require me' Mustafa said, gesturing towards a small café to the right, where men sat drinking tea and played backgammon. 'Happy shopping' he added as he headed towards the café for his sweet fix.

The rest of the party spilt into couples and small groups. I had to admit, I felt a little anxious. I was alone and I'd finally accepted it.

The smell of mint and cumin hit me. It seemed that this part was home to the spice stalls. Pyramids of spices were perched amongst dried chillies, figs and apricots. Jars filled with cinnamon and tea leaves lined the shelves behind. Sellers were shouting in an attempt to sell their goods. I was tempted but I wasn't in need of spices of any kind – I'd bought enough. I longed for a house lined with orange trees and a spice garden just outside the kitchen window but right now that was a distant dream. I told myself no once more as

13

I passed walnut stuffed dates. I needed to take a break from the sweet indulgences, all of them. I walked deeper into the market and came to a cross road. This really is a maze. I turned left, following the arched ceilings and wooden beams overhead. Ornately painted bowls and vases hung from these. The detail was truly breathtaking. I admired the blemishes on the clay pots, not one single piece alike.

Travelling into the heart of the bazaar, I passed everything from leather and fur goods to hand stitched, silk rugs and elaborate costume jewellery. The deeper I walked, the hotter it became. Hundreds of bodies pushed in different directions to find what they thought to be a bargain. I'd since lost all sense of direction yet there was still plenty of time. I made another right turn, avoiding a crowd ahead. Glass lanterns, decorated with jewelled mosaics, hung from the ceiling. Each one housed a candle, lighting the darkened path ahead. Amber and emerald flooded the stoned street and twinkled like fairy lights. The little bit of magic that I was after perhaps?

Then something caught my sight. It was a deep blue, swirling into a clearer shade before ending in darkness. This was no shard of mosaic. The eyes stared at me through the hanging lanterns. I stood there, mesmerised. Then, I caught glimpse of to whom they belonged.

Chapter Two

He was staring. His eyes barely even blinked. What was he looking at? I glanced over my shoulder to find only brickwork behind. It must be me. He was fairly tall, sporting a muscular torso. Thick, dark hair covered his head whilst stubble coated his face. He wore a black shirt, partly unbuttoned and turned up at the cuff, revealing his olive skin and dark chest hair. Leaning against the stone wall, his hands rested in the pockets of his denim jeans. He was still staring, smirking.

I'd never had much luck with men. I'm twenty four and had only loved twice. Love – I can only guess that's what it was anyway. Samuel was my first kiss at sixteen whom had lost interest after we had done the deed. We were only kids though. And then there was Mark. Where do I begin? I met

Mark at university and I fell for him at first sight. He was older than I was and quite the romancer. He was handsome but he knew it. I was head over heels in love with his witty charm after only a few dates. The other girls – yes there were plenty – must have loved the endless gifts but I've always been a hopeless romantic, well hopeful I guess. I'd take a loving kiss over a designer purse any day of the week – and this was me talking. Mark didn't do love, well true love anyway. He'd break your heart and then try to fix it with a pair of Chanel sunglasses. It worked at the beginning but over the years I couldn't take any more heartache from one man, hence the impulse travelling. Come to think of it, I hadn't heard from Mark for months now. We'd been over for the best part of a year yet he'd always worm his way back into my life. I'd thought perhaps if I left the ordinary life then he too would fade away with it but he was still there at the back of my mind. He would always call me beautiful but now I questioned that very word. It was another lie. He had royally screwed me up.

The mystery man walked towards me. Who was he? What did he want? I twisted the ends of my hair – something I did instinctively when I was nervous. He was now standing about a foot away from me. Wow, he was even more handsome up close. His lips parted, revealing his faultless smile as he inhaled slightly to speak.

'Hi' he said.

'Hello' I replied, still slightly on edge.

'What's your name?' he asked. His voice was deep, charmingly so.

'Rose' I whispered.

'Rose' he repeated, rolling the r slightly.

I had always been partial to a foreign accent yet the way he curved his tongue around my name made me weak.

'You are a true beauty' he added.

There it was. I couldn't help but roll my eyes.

'You don't think yes?' he asked. His English was a little off but that seemed to add to his charm.

'Onur' he said, holding out his hand.

It's nice to meet you' I replied.

I winced as the words left my mouth. I'd never been the flirtatious type and didn't have a clue about chat-up lines. Kelly – my friend from school – always knew exactly what to say. She'd flutter her long lashes, pout her lips, the boys would come running and she'd pick from the line up. She was confident and well, that just wasn't me. Yes, I was happy with the way I looked but that was mainly down to the clothes. I'd speak to a guy on a night out but after making small talk for a matter of minutes, he'd eye up the girl passing by. I mean, who wants to talk about literature and fairy-tale endings anyway? I was still waiting for the answer to that question.

'Nice?' he asked with a smirk.

He seemed full of himself, another Mark perhaps. I refrained from rolling my eyes a second time. That would be bad manners.

'What brings you here?' he then asked.

Why was I even speaking to this stranger? Walk away. I couldn't. I was intrigued and we weren't technically strangers anymore. I never did answer his question though. He must have realised that he was getting nowhere with the general chit-chat.

'You want one?' he asked, gesturing towards the lanterns which I had since forgotten about.

'Yes, they're beautiful' I replied.

He inhaled to speak but seemed to stop himself – perhaps another comment about my so-called beauty. He brushed his fingers across the array of mosaic tiles. He wore a thick gold band on his index finger. His ring finger was bare. I don't know why I picked up on that. Moments passed before he reached for a lantern.

'This one' he said – a statement rather than a question.

The lantern was charcoal grey, embellished with jade gems in the shape of a sun. Red mosaic shards decorated the corners. It was unique. I took the lantern from his grasp and handed it to the merchant who was watching us, intently so. The sooner I bought it, the sooner I could leave.

'How much is it?' I asked.

'Three hundred' the merchant replied.

I began to rummage in my tote for my purse. Onur then spoke. I couldn't understand a word of what was being said but their raised voices and body language told me that they weren't discussing the weather. I stood there, my eyes flitting back and to. Onur then handed a fifty to the seller. This was haggling it seemed. The seller wrapped the lantern in white tissue paper before handing it to me. I glanced at Onur and he winked, baring his beautiful smile once more. I'd known this man all of two minutes and he was already buying me gifts. I questioned his intentions.

"Beautiful, like you" he said, smirking.

He just couldn't resist himself. His intentions were probably somewhat dishonourable but this time I couldn't help but smile.

I checked my wrist for the time. I had another thirty minutes or so. I wondered how long it would take to find my way back through the maze.

'You like coffee?' Onur asked, interrupting my thoughts.

This wasn't a simple question but more of an invitation. I replied *yes* anyway. He started to walk down the narrow passageway. I guess he wanted me to follow him so I did. We walked side by side in silence. He would occasionally glance at me and I would do the same. Rose, what are you doing? I was following a man I hardly knew deeper into a maze. I couldn't fall for another man, another Mark. Still, I followed his every move. I couldn't stop myself but, more importantly, I didn't want to. There was just something about him.

We came to an opening in the stone wall which housed a stairway. He said nothing but gestured his hand towards the stairs, allowing me to go first. The opening was extremely narrow, the marble steps warped slightly. The walls either side were tiled in every shade of blue. A tarnished, bronze chandelier hung from the low ceiling. I bowed my head to pass. I was a trusting person. I had never even asked where we were going – for coffee I suppose. The right turn at the top of the stairs lead into a small square room with half a dozen wooden tables and chairs. There was no one else here. A large window photographed the street of the bazaar. He gestured for me to choose a table. I sat down at the table next to the window and Onur joined me, reclining in his chair. A petite waitress came over. She was pretty.

'*Hoşgeldiniz*' she said.

I'd heard this word once or twice now. I wasn't certain but I took it to mean welcome.

Onur proceeded to speak to the girl in his native tongue before pausing to ask 'What would you like?'

'Coffee please' I replied.

'Sweet?' he asked.

I nodded. He turned back to the girl and said something else in Turkish. She cast me a look before turning away. There appeared to be jealousy in her gaze and I wasn't sure why.

'I know your name but I want to know more' he said.

Here we go. He charms me and now wants more. I was reluctant to roll my eyes.

'More?' I asked, naively.

The waitress was back at our table in a flash, this time holding two small cups. She put them down, staring at me yet again.

'*Sağol*' I said and Onur looked at me in amazement. I gave myself an imaginary high five.

What looked like an espresso now sat in front of me. The cup and saucer were beautifully painted with a white and pale blue pattern. I took a sip. Wow, that is sweet. The coffee was slightly muddy in consistency. Two gulps later, I was greeted with a thick substance. Barely even coffee if you ask me. I much preferred a *café crème* but I wasn't in Paris now.

'Don't drink all' ordered Onur. I looked at him blankly.

'Trust me' he replied smugly.

I had to admit, I didn't like being told what to do. Mark had always bossed me around. Do this and do that. I paused, reluctantly. Onur held my gaze and I did in fact place it down. He reached for the cup and turned it over, a little coffee spilling onto the saucer.

'Wait' he instructed.

He was still staring at me. I couldn't begin to imagine what I looked like. The humidity wasn't my friend that's for sure. I could feel the hair at the nape of my neck curling from the heat. We sat there in silence. Moments later he reached out. I thought he was going to touch my hand and my heartbeat quickened. Instead, he reached for the cup. He turned it upright and inspected the inside.

'Who is Rose?' he asked. I was still none the wiser.

He put the cup down and laughed. 'It is, how you say, fortune seeing?'

'Fortune-telling' I corrected. 'So what does my future hold?'

I'd always wanted someone to read my palms but I feared the truth.

He paused. 'Yours is not certain' he then replied.

I could have told myself that. Perhaps it was a load of superstitious nonsense but his smile, well that was genuine enough. He seemed happy to be in my company and I didn't have to keep him interested. The waitress walked by and his eyes never moved. This was new to me. It was warming. I smiled back at him, into those blue eyes. What was it about him? I couldn't put my finger on it. He seemed different to those guys in the bars. It wasn't quite literature and fairy tales but it was close. Was Mum right, could he be that *someone*? I sounded ridiculous. I'd only known him a matter of minutes. I looked at the time. I should have been at the café more than ten minutes ago.

'I have to go' I exclaimed.

He frowned, looking at me blankly.

'I'm sorry' I said as ran towards the stairs.

It was a tad dramatic. I felt like Cinderella at the stroke of midnight. Well, minus the glass slippers and fairy godmother of course.

'Wait' he called. He ran after me and grabbed my hand. 'I will take you.'

We dashed down the marble steps and were once again in the heart of the bustling bazaar. He knew his way around. This must have been home for him but I hadn't bothered to ask. Come to think of it, I hadn't asked him anything. I only knew his name, and he only knew mine. Yet the unknown was somewhat captivating. I lost track of the endless turns. There must have been some sort of shortcut to the maze as it was only a matter of minutes before we saw daylight. I could see Mustafa, along with his umbrella, in front of the café.

'I have to go now' I said as I removed my hand from his grip. He no longer held a smile.

'Goodbye' I said. The word was so final.

'Goodbye?' he retorted. The smug smile was back. 'This is not goodbye.'

I smiled at his persistency. I searched in my tote to find the card which I had taken from the hotel reception earlier that day and handed it to him. It was a little fast but I needed to live a little. He put his arm around my waist and pulled me close, lifting me slightly to meet his height. Our bodies touching, his breath was on mine. He smelt of cigarettes and oaky vanilla – perhaps his aftershave. His grip tightened around my waist, his other hand now caressing my hair. He gazed into my eyes. The blue iris of his looked more sapphire now. Then, in one swift move, he parted his lips and pressed them to mine. I closed my eyes as his tongue searched my mouth. I could taste the sweetness of the coffee mixed with the bitterness of tobacco. Then, he pulled away. The taste lingered upon my now tender lips. His breath warm, he whispered something in my ear.

'*Gülüm*' he said.

I held onto that one word, unbeknown to me, as he let go.

Chapter Three

What had just happened? Who was he? Besides his name, I knew nothing about him. I brushed my fingers across my now inflamed lips. His tender kiss had stained them. The intensity of the moment lingered. I looked up and there he was, in the distance. He cast one last smile my way and then he was gone.

It was one moment of passion Rose, that's all. It meant nothing. I'd never been kissed like that before. It had been a while. Sam used to stick his tongue down my throat – he had no idea. And Mark, well he'd rather do other things than just kiss. Onur was something else. It was like I'd been kissed for the first time. I was sixteen and smitten with romance once more.

It was late afternoon now. The heat was more bearable, the sun slightly lower. Some merchants were packing up their goods for the day whilst others continued to entice customers. I hurried across the cobbled streets, ignoring the calls of the traders. Mustafa caught sight of me and beckoned me over. They must have been waiting for at least half an hour by now. The group shot me looks of annoyance.

'I'm so sorry, I-' I muttered.

'There is no need to apologise my dear' Mustafa said before I could finish.

I smiled at him in gratitude. He brushed the pastry crumbs from his cotton shirt and licked the coffee stains from his lips before gesturing towards the path ahead. We followed him as he wandered through the narrow lanes. I walked beside him. Faint whispers were audible from behind. I too would have been annoyed. Then again, I could have been lost in the maze or worse kidnapped. Not that any of them cared. That's the way of the world, people look out for number one as it seems.

The buildings down this street were white and terracotta with red wooden shutters, the paint chipped. Housewives chatted outside as they hung their washing overhead. I bowed my head as we passed. The smell of Turkish home cooking drifted through the streets. This district offered an insight into the everyday life of the city. There was much to be appreciated yet I was otherwise occupied with the thought of another.

I had no idea what it meant but I was mesmerised by that one word. There had been passion in his voice. I savoured the moment and our heated embrace.

'Did you manage to haggle?' Mustafa asked, interrupting my thoughts.

'Sorry?' I asked.

He gestured towards the item in my hand. He hadn't engaged in small talk until now. Perhaps he felt sorry for me? That's what seems to happen when you're alone.

'Oh yes. It's a lantern' I answered.

'This city is filled with things which are pleasing to the eye' he then said with a slight grin.

It seemed a little too apt. Had he caught sight of that moment? I began to twist my hair, my cheeks now crimson, as I simply nodded in response.

'The unknown can be enchanting' he added.

He had a way with words. This could have been taken one of two ways – a subtle warning or a chance and meaningless statement. I opted for the latter. I gazed forwards, not wishing to acknowledge the possible implications and went back to my lust-stricken thoughts.

The narrow streets opened. Trams signalled their presence and countless taxis sped past. We were now standing in the midst of the square from where we had come hours before. The sun now rested on the dome of the mosque. Birds perched upon it, their silhouettes reflected onto the pavement. This city was breathtaking in any light.

The beauty would be radiated even in darkness. Mustafa began to cross the road, cars swerving around him.

'Follow me please' he casually ordered as he raised his umbrella in the air.

The group scurried across the road to join him on the other side. I looked down at my sandals - probably not the best choice of footwear I had to admit. They were pretty though. Even so, running wasn't my style. I stood on the edge of the pavement, debating when to cross. I caught a girl in our group rolling her eyes. Vehicles sounded their horns as I weaved in and out of the traffic. Traffic lights didn't seem to matter here, neither did road markings. I managed to get across in one piece.

The street vendor next to us was selling sesame crusted baked goods twisted into what looked like a bagel. I loved the smell of fresh bread. I hadn't eaten since breakfast and even then I'd hardly had a lot. Mustafa had had his sweet fix at the café and the others presumably had eaten whilst I was otherwise engaged. I blushed. All I could think about was food. That's always the way isn't it? You can go for hours without eating anything and then all of a sudden you become ravenous. I rarely ate a lot back home. Once I'd spent my loan on labels, there wasn't much left for the weekly shop. Mark had wined and dined me. Mustafa had been speaking about history for some time. I hadn't really been listening so another minute couldn't hurt. I walked over to one of the carts. The seller smiled as I approached. I thought it best not to speak so I simply pointed. It's remarkable how much you can convey through body language. He nodded and put the bagel-like goods into a paper bag, printed with the word *simit*. I placed a few coins in his hand and he handed the bag to me. It was delicious. The saltiness of the crust flattered the soft dough inside, the sesame seeds adding texture. No wonder this was popular. I joined the group again, enjoying the baked goods as Mustafa spoke.

'*Yerebatan Sarnıcı.* The famed Basilica Cistern' he stated.

I frowned. The building which stood before us was nothing of significance. It was a single storey with brick exterior and barred windows. I was underwhelmed. I must have missed something.

'The largest of the several hundred ancient cisterns' Mustafa continued as we entered.

It was dark. There were a few little shops, selling primarily postcards and fridge magnets – the usual tack you would expect to find in tourist areas. We passed these. There was a flight of wooden steps at the end of the corridor.

'Follow me please as we enter the cistern' said Mustafa.

We followed him in single file down the narrow passageway. The wooden planks creaked with each step. I wondered the age of this so-called wonder. The stairway opened ahead. I was overwhelmed at the concealed beauty which lay beneath the city. It was vast. Rows of stone columns supported the arched ceilings above. Intricate, marble detailing decorated these. The darkness was lit by candles and dimmed floor lighting. Wooden planks lined the edges. The gaps revealed the water beneath. They say don't judge a book by its cover and it's true.

I began to walk across the wooden floors, listening to the gentle movement of the water below. It was tranquil. There were many signs stating the history, building on what Mustafa had already said. There was a gathering of people ahead. I waited in turn, making my way to the front. There was a column with a large base, partly submerged in the water. It was carved with the face of Medusa. It said that the base is inverted to prevent the power of the Gorgon's gaze – a Greek myth. Could a gaze really be that powerful? It seemed it could. I just couldn't forget the blue-eyed boy.

I wandered around the perimeter of the cistern, gazing up into the vast archways overhead. I'd had enough history for one day. It was the first time that I'd felt lonely. How ironic. I'd been travelling for months now with only myself as company and after one sweet indulgence I'd become addicted, hooked on a man I didn't even know.

It was dusk outside. The sun was absent, the sky now a deep red fading into darkness across the land. The temperature had dropped yet it was still warm. I closed my eyes, listening to the hum of the passing traffic. The scent of tobacco filled the air. I looked right to see Mustafa smoking a cigar. He reminded me of my grandfather, a kind soul who enjoyed puffing on his pipe whilst reading the morning paper. Beneath the wisdom, Mustafa seemed to enjoy the simplicities in life. I admired him. He glanced my way and walked over to me.

'Do you smoke?' he asked, offering a cigar my way.

I shook my head. I'd once tried a cigarette in my teens but despised that bitter aftertaste. He seemed to approve, smiling as he blew the smoke in the opposite direction.

'So, what are your thoughts on her?' he then asked. I presumed he was speaking of the city.

'She is breathtaking' I replied.

He smiled. 'You are yet to see her full beauty' he added. 'How long are you planning to stay?'

'One week. Although it doesn't seem long enough' I said, slightly saddened.

'Savour her every moment my dear' he added.

Members of the group soon began to filter back. Mustafa then spoke to us all.

'Ladies and gentlemen, we now come to the end of our tour. I can only hope that you now share the same love for the city which I myself do. Before we part ways, I wish you good fortune for the rest of your journey.' He placed his hand over his chest, lowering his head slightly.

We walked slowly through the cobbled streets, leaving several of our party at their hotels along the way. The city had a different tone in the evening. The vendors and artists whom lined the streets during the day had since disappeared. This place seemed to come alive in this hour. Musicians serenaded onlookers with their stringed instruments whilst others sold flowers to budding new couples. Street lights illuminated the roads and candles flickered in the distance. Nearby bars and restaurants were thriving, the smell of slow roasted spices and grilled meats flooded the air. It truly was beautiful in any light.

We soon stopped once more as the last couple arrived at their hotel. Mustafa escorted them inside whilst I breathed in the charm of the city.

'Shall we?' he said one last time as we walked down a narrow side street.

It was just us two. There was an awkward silence for a little while before he spoke.

'What fate has brought you here Rose?'

It was question which even I myself didn't know the answer to. I shrugged in response.

'She will always be my home. I am a lucky man' he said. 'One day I'm sure you'll find that something you've been looking for.'

He continued to speak about the wonders which he had visited in his lifetime but his voice soon became a background noise. I was fixated upon finding myself over these past months – whatever that even means – not finding something. The thought settled in my mind. Was I searching for something or simply someone? I was a mess. I didn't know what I wanted. I'd waited tables for almost a year after graduation, debating what to do with my life. Teaching, journalism – I was still none the wiser. I always knew exactly what I wanted to be when I grew up but the magic seems to fade when you reach a certain age. I couldn't settle for ordinary. There had to be more.

Mustafa stopped. I gazed up at the quaint hotel which I had left earlier today – a lifetime ago, or so it felt like it. I admired the delicate pink flowers in boxes underneath the shuttered windows.

'It has been a pleasure my dear' he spoke, bowing his head in gratitude.

His eyes smiled, the chocolate irises sparkled in the street lights. He turned on his heel, using his umbrella to guide him through the uneven cobbles. I'd never asked him anything about his life yet I held such visions of it. It's strange to think that many of those whom we meet remain somewhat strangers to us. He disappeared into the heart of the old quarter once more.

'*İyi akşamlar*' spoke the man behind reception.

I admired the accent. It wasn't as harsh as Arabic, slightly softer but fascinating nevertheless. I didn't understand but I smiled in response. I glanced around the foyer. The chairs were empty, the newspapers untouched. Did I really expect him to be here? I felt disappointed and slightly embarrassed as I walked onwards to my room.

The soles of my feet were throbbing. I looked at my sandals – definitely not the best choice of footwear. Pain is beauty. I opened the door, met with the scent of lavender and fresh bedding. I took a deep breath. I loved having the bed to myself. I'd always thought a man would wrap his arms around you after sex but that's another lie. Mark always said he wasn't the cuddling type. There lay a silver dish on the bedside table filled with rose Turkish delight. An oil lantern lit the room. Pink petals, like those underneath the windows, were dusted across the bathroom tiles. An array of bath salts and oils lined the claw-foot bath tub. There was a letter on the desk in the corner of the room. It was from the concierge.

'Dear Ms Jones,
This was delivered for you earlier today with the
accompanying note.
Regards'

On the oak desk lay a single red rose. It was a deep crimson, each petal symmetrical. Resting on the stem was a card, holding one word, that word. I turned it over, my hands shaking. The reverse held another message:

'This is not goodbye.'

It was surreal, something you would expect to find in the pages of a love story. It was the loving gesture which I had always craved – inexpensive yet heartfelt. I couldn't seem to rid the smile which now beamed across my face. If this isn't goodbye then when will we meet again? I'd always been a little too organised. Not a live for the moment kind of girl. I hated impromptu dates but this was exciting. Mustafa was right, the unknown is enchanting. I'd just have to wait. I couldn't chase him. Even if I wanted to, I didn't know where he'd be but he knew where I was.

I reached for the bath salts, dusting them into the running water and undressed. The bead pinned to the scarf caught my gaze. *The blue eye protects against evil.* I dimmed the lightening so only the flicker of the lantern filled the room. I breathed in the fragrance as I stepped into the heated water, soothing my tired body. I closed my eyes. If only his blue eyes would protect me. Now what a thought that was.

Chapter Four

What a dream. I'd seen the dreamboat and how dreamy he was. There was just something about him. He was romantic – a little cliché perhaps – and handsome. I touched my lips, longing for another kiss. I was giddy. That's enough Rose. It was just a dream. Light ran through the open window and gentle bird song filled the air. The room was cool. I inhaled the scent of lavender upon the sheets. The candles had since burned out but the fragrance lingered. It was another day and I only hoped I'd see him.

I'd missed a call from Eve, Evelyn – a true friend since childhood. We hadn't seen each other for months but somehow, even from half a world away, we were just as close as ever. Thank goodness for video calls. I'd love to write letters to those I loved from across the ocean but the reality was a little different. No one sends letters anymore. Even birthday wishes are sent half heartedly by text nowadays. There was just something about a handwritten letter – a person's signature asserting their love. *Love*

Letters of Great Men had always been a favourite of mine. The pages were filled with nothing but love, even amid war and sorrow. Eve and I said we'd send letters to each other but we never had. I had always been slightly jealous of Eve. She was a homeowner, of a charming house I might add, married to a loving man and had a beautiful baby in tow. She had her life together. And if that wasn't enough, she was blessed with glossy brown locks and a bubbly personality which everyone adored. And where was I? I was unemployed with student debts around my neck, single and backpacking alone to forget the "love" which had hurt me so deeply. It was clear that my life was anything but together. I sighed. I'll ring her later. There were other messages – a lengthy one from Mum included. I didn't have the heart to begin replying now.

I nested into the goose down goodness for a little longer. The rose petals caught my sight. It wasn't a dream, it had happened. I searched that one word, my heart racing. The internet was slow and I was as ever impatient. I was nervous, intrigued perhaps. The translation came upon the screen – *my rose*. I was his. I couldn't rid my smile. I was love drunk from a man I hardly knew. It was laughable really, a fleeting romance. I'd wasted years of my life analysing my relationship, if you could even call it that, and this time I just didn't care. He'd made me smile if nothing else.

I flung back the sheets and skipped to the bathroom. How one little thing can make your day. I washed my face, applied a little mascara to my lashes and brushed a nude across my lips. I wasn't one of these girls to cake their face in make-up. It wasn't my style. I much preferred the natural look. I scrunched my damp hair with coconut oil and the loose curls ran down my back. I wore a champagne coloured slip and paired it with an Aspinal of London bag – another gift. I loved the brand. It was quintessentially British and the pieces were timeless. I was yet to see a fake and I'd seen a lot of knock-offs that's for sure. They were a fraction of the price but owning a Louis Vuitton with 'Made in China' stitched into the lining didn't seem right. I'd wanted this bag for months – it was evergreen croc leather with gold clasps. I'd worked extra shifts at the restaurant to buy it but Mark had swan in and bought it for me. Money was no object for Mark. He owned his own business. Well, that's what he told people, including me. Truth be told, he'd inherited it from his millionaire grandfather. I had relished in the expensive lifestyle at first but it soon became boring and somewhat predictable. Mark hadn't done an honest day's work in his life. Instead, he sat back and watched Daddy Warbucks' money roll in. That was half the problem. Mark would use his wealth to apologise or declare his so-called love. I soon lost sight of true romance and knew that the lifestyle wasn't for me. I kept the bag. It would be rude not to.

I had no plans for the day. I waited for the elevator and a middle aged man joined me. The doors opened and he gestured, allowing me to enter first. How courteous. There are few men like this left in the world. He reminded me of my father, a true gentleman whose kindness couldn't possibly be measured. I began to think of home.

'How much?' he asked.

'Sorry?' I said, turning to face him.

'How much?' he repeated, raising his brows a little.

I shrugged, still none the wiser. He became flustered and dashed out at the next floor. It took me a minute but surely not. I looked at myself in the mirror. Nothing screamed prostitute about this outfit. What a fabulous start to the day.

The doors opened onto the terrace and the heat hit me. I took a seat at a table beside the balcony. I was once again taken aback by the beauty. The terrace photographed the skyline of Istanbul. The sun painted silhouettes of the mosques and the clouds created a haze over the tree tops. The sounds were enchanting. There was the calls of merchants, the hum of traffic and the beloved call to prayer. I admired the grey and blue charm of the building in front, along with the crisp white petals which lined the gardens below.

'Coffee?' posed a waiter. It was the same chap as the day before.

'Tea?' I asked.

Strong coffee was the last thing on my mind and I had no desire to see my fortune in a cup today. He nodded and turned on his heel. I took a few snaps of the view. He was back in a flash, placing a glass on the table. It was shaped like a tulip, the rim wide enough to simply hold between your fingers. There was no milk in sight. No one overseas understood the concept of a milky cup of tea. The Brit inside me sighed.

'Are you ready to order Madam?' asked the waiter.

I wasn't sure what I wanted – the story of my life as it seemed. I scanned over the menu and pointed to a dish named *menemen* without further ado. He smiled and noted it down.

I felt my phone vibrate, yet again. It was another pointless notification. Everyone shared the intimacies of their lives on social media nowadays. I remember when life was simpler. I'd knock on my friend's door or call the house phone but things change. I'd grown tired of changing my relationship status from 'it's complicated' to 'single' time and time again. I'd spend hours aimlessly scrolling through feeds which I wasn't necessarily interested in but because it was the thing to do. I turned it off. I needed a break from the outside world. I wanted the simple life.

It wasn't long before the waiter served my breakfast. It was a copper pan filled with scrambled eggs, tomatoes and green peppers. I took a mouthful. The oregano and ground black pepper added depth to an otherwise simple dish. It was delicious. I turned towards the sun, inhaling the light.

I soon lost track of how long I'd been sitting there. My pale skin was now a faint red in colour. It would be wise to get out of the midday sun. Taking the lift down to the foyer, I felt nauseous. I checked my appearance in the mirror and applied a little lipstick. I was slightly rosy now. I smiled at those waiting as the doors opened but they seemed reluctant to smile back. I'd always manage a cheery hello in London but it wasn't the norm here. Perhaps a cheery hello labels you as a hooker here. I blushed. The chairs were empty and the papers still untouched. I walked over to the front desk.

'Good morning Madam' said the man behind reception. He was quite young – earning pennies through the summer holidays perhaps.

'How can I help?' he asked.

'Are there any messages for me, Rose Jones?' I asked, hopefully.

'Please may I have your room number?' he said.

'213' I answered.

'One moment please' he said, turning to search through the envelopes behind him.

I bit my lip in anticipation.

'There are no messages Madam. Can I help with anything else?' he then asked.

Of course there weren't any messages. This wasn't a fairy tale, this was real life. I'd half expected Onur to be waiting with a dozen red roses and we would kiss passionately, living happily ever after. Oh how silly I sounded. I asked for some information on excursions of the city. I flicked through the glossy pages, it wasn't quite *Vogue*, and stepped outside.

'Taxi?' asked the porter.

I nodded, thanking him as he opened the door. There were a few museums listed which caught my eye. Fine art had always been one of my obsessions. That's what Paris does to you. I remember standing in the midst of The Louvre, gazing up at the intricate brush strokes of the paintings overhead. There was one painting in particular. Pale blue oil paints were dabbed with ivory, depicting serenity. Monet stole my heart. Paris had to be the most romantic city in the world. I'd wanted to live there since I was a dot. I'd dreamed of reading poetry by the Seine whilst I leaned into the man I loved – cliché I know. We'd eat baguette and brie upon a bench in The Tuileries Garden. Life would be magical. I shook my head and slid into the taxi. I pointed to a museum in the leaflet – *Ayasofya Müzesi*. He nodded and sped past the other taxis.

The city was in its prime once more – bustling streets, roaring trades and hectic traffic queues. It amazed me how one city could be so tranquil yet so chaotic. The traffic halted yet again. There was no air conditioning, or air for that matter, in this taxi. I looked in my bag for a fan. It was beautiful – a gift from a friend's travels to India – ivory lace across a wooden frame. I admired it as I frantically fanned my face. Slightly cooler, I gazed out of the window. There was a woman walking on the footpath, alongside the traffic. Her face and body were covered in embroidered cloth. She was holding hands with her daughter. She was a beautiful girl with dark ringlets and tanned skin dressed in pale pink. The little girl was skipping, smiling infectiously. The woman looked down at her, her eyes filled with love. I couldn't help but smile. The love in her gaze was warming. They say that meaning can be lost in translation, yet in that very moment I saw that love is a concept apparent across the languages.

The taxi stopped. The surroundings looked somewhat familiar. The driver mumbled something or other and gestured outside. I gave him a few notes – too much – but he didn't give me any change. Oh well, I wasn't going to quibble over a few coins.

I was standing in the heart of the old quarter once more. I wanted to double check that I was in the right place but he'd since driven away. I walked towards the building in front of me. It lay opposite The Blue Mosque, mirroring the grandeur. Fountains lay in between, the water creating archways, framing the view. The building was painted a rusty red with grey domed roofs and chrome detailing. The faded exterior mirrored its age. There was a small queue outside which I joined. Ivy embellished the wall to my left and greenery shaded the path where I stood. It wasn't long before I moved inside.

The interior was something else. Grand chandeliers hung from the vast ceilings, warming the cold stone floors. The gold painted walls were faded, crumbling slightly, but the images mesmerising nonetheless. Arched windows allowed light to fill the domes overhead. I closed my eyes as the sunlight warmed my face. There were many tours ahead. It was hard not to overhear the tour guides in such close proximity. I absorbed any information I could, admiring the history of this once Orthodox basilica – according to the gentleman ahead.

Artwork depicting renowned scholars and poets painted the walls. The arts had always been a weakness of mine. I had spent countless nights lost in the pages of English literature. The hopeless romantics of the nineteenth century wooed my heart. Those years were spent awaiting my very own Mr. Darcy – the fairy-tale ending that every girl is promised. I went on to study the literature which I was so very fond of. And then I met my Mr. Right, or so I thought. Never did I think that the so-called Prince Charming in my story would have his way with countless other maidens. We didn't live happily ever after that's for sure. I had longed to become a writer but I'd since lost sight of true romance. How was I to write about falling in love when I didn't even know how? Heartbroken, twice, I left it all behind me. Present day and it now seemed that a new character held a spell over me. I longed for the fairy tale, any girl did, but I was reluctant to believe that we would fly into the distance together on a magic carpet.

I meandered around the museum, questioning my past and contemplating my future. I used to be so sure of what I wanted but now I was clueless. It's not the norm to have everything figured out by the time you're twenty anymore. But I wasn't twenty. I was twenty four, closer to twenty five. Where does the time go? It's true that travel does broaden one's mind but I would trade it all for that happy ever after.

It wasn't long before I decided to leave. The sun was lower now, bleeding into the clouds overhead. I didn't want to stay out too late, alone in a big city. I sighed at the thought. Oh how I'd love to share this with my other half, or anyone for that matter. And it was then that I'd never felt more alone. I hailed a taxi. I showed the hotel address to the driver. He was middle aged, overweight and smelt of cigarettes and kebabs. He nodded, joining the traffic.

We pulled up outside of the hotel in what seemed like a matter of seconds. I must have been away with the fairies. I passed the driver a few notes and he actually gave me change. He then stepped out to open the door for me – something I rarely saw in this day and age. I stood on the cobbled street as he drove into the distance. There was a slight breeze now, my skin cool against the silk. I turned to face the hotel and inhaled sharply.

It was him. The man I couldn't seem to rid from my thoughts. He was leaning against the brick exterior, one foot pressed against the wall. He had a cigarette in his hand, exhaling the smoke across his parted lips. I could still feel their touch upon mine, paired with the taste of tobacco. I bit my once tender lips at the thought. He wore a white tailored shirt, unbuttoned slightly yet again, and black trousers. He was undeniably handsome. I took a deep breath as my heartbeat quickened, unable to move my gaze. Then, his eyes met mine. They warmed my skin instantly. He smiled as he threw his cigarette to the floor and walked towards me.

Chapter Five

"Hello Rose" he said softly, his body inches away from mine.

'Hi' I whispered.

I still couldn't seem to work him out. He looked smug, self-assured somehow. I was mesmerised nonetheless. He looked into my eyes as his glimmered against the subdued streetlight. I lost myself in his gaze. They say a person's eyes are a window to their soul and if his were anything to go by then I couldn't imagine how wonderful he truly was. We stood there in silence for some time. I'd be damned if I was going to speak first. What would I even say? I knew nothing of the man standing inches away from me. He was so familiar yet so foreign at the same time – no wonder I was fascinated. And then, he spoke.

'I have been thinking of you' he said, edging closer. It was close enough to taste the tobacco upon his lips.

I'd thought about nothing other than him. How could I admit that? I'd sound desperate. I said nothing and twisted the ends of my hair. His smirk faded as he awaited a reply.

'This evening, what will you do?' he then asked, straight to the point.

I was taken aback. I had no plans whatsoever and longed to spend the evening with my mystery man. It would be an adventure.

'Good. You will spend tonight with me' he said.

I hadn't even answered his question yet he had assumed the response. It was the right answer but still. Was I really that transparent? The smirk was back again. He was sure of himself, now that was obvious. I wanted to throw the offer in his face but I couldn't bring myself to do so. I wanted him.

'Come' he ordered and reached out for my hand.

Surely not right now. God only knows what I looked like.

'Wait. Where are we going?' I asked, anxiously.

'You will see' he replied, smirking once more.

He grabbed my hand, gently pressing my palm. His touch was warming. He whistled for a taxi. He pulled me towards him, gripping my waist. Only the silk of my dress stood in the way of our bare skin. I inhaled sharply, inches away from his parted lips. He teased me as he leaned closer and held me tight. My body arched, meeting his. I wanted him. I hadn't felt a man's touch since Mark. I was probably a re-born virgin by now. Who was I kidding, I was desperate. Onur came closer, opening the door and gestured for me to enter. He winked as I slid inside. I felt frustrated, longing for his touch. He spoke to the driver and the taxi pulled away, turning down yet another side street. This city really is a maze I thought as we sped down the endless winding paths.

Onur engaged in friendly chit-chat, or so it seemed, with the driver. I had never felt more on edge in my life. He was insanely gorgeous, the type of guy you would find posing for a perfume ad in *Vogue* – completely out of my league. And what's more, I had no idea where he was taking me or what he was even saying for that matter. I caught sight of myself in the rear-view mirror. It was early evening now, my curls had dropped a little and my face was shiny from the heat of the city. I had to admit, I didn't look too bad. Onur's hand rested upon my leg, caressing it ever so slightly. The sensation of his touch sent shivers across my skin. I bit my lip to refrain from reacting.

'So...' I began. The word had left my mouth and I had no idea how to follow it.

'So?' He questioned, frowning.

'Are you from here?' I then asked.

It was all I could think of, well apart from '*Are you single?*' and '*Will you marry me?*' that is. He had this seductive thing going on and I had to ruin it with my boring questions. It probably wouldn't be long before he was eyeing up the next girl.

'No' he replied. 'Home is far from here.'

He gave nothing away. I twirled my fingers, knotting my hair. I knew what he wanted. He'd have his way with the girl passing through town. He'd never have to call her. There would be no strings attached.

'What about Rose? Where is your home?' he asked.

'London' I answered. I too was giving away as little as he was.

'An English Rose' he then said.

It was a cheesy chat-up line but it made me smile. I couldn't work this guy out. He was arrogant, mysterious and sweet all in one.

I gazed out of the window. The sun has set in the distance and darkness filled the sky. I didn't recognise anything outside. It was difficult to tell in this light. We drove across a vast iron bridge. We'd only be travelling for ten minutes or so but it felt like days. Onur put his arm around me and I lost myself in his embrace. There it was again, the scent of vanilla. I cast my mind back to our first encounter. I leaned against him and closed my eyes. Could he be my Mr. Right? I sounded ridiculous but it did seem like a real life fairy tale. We rode in silence for the rest of the journey. I felt at ease next to him. There was no awkwardness, just two strangers content in each other's company.

The taxi stopped. I must have slept.

'Rose?' whispered Onur. I still loved the way he curled his tongue around my name.

'Yes' I replied, sitting up and smoothing my hair.

'We are here' he said softly.

He stepped out of the taxi, holding out his hand to take mine. The city was bustling here. Market stalls were thriving even at this hour, musicians playing their instruments whilst merchants shouted to attract onlookers. I clung to Onur. It was dark and a little overwhelming. I squeezed his hand and he pulled me close as we weaved in and out of the crowds ahead.

We soon came to the edge of the cobbled street, nothing but darkness ahead. The breeze stroked my skin. I hadn't noticed until now but it was cold. I took the shawl from my bag and wrapped the cloth around my bare shoulders. Onur pulled me close to his chest, his arms around me. We stood there in silence. I searched his face as he gazed into the distance. It was quite nice to just stand next to him, no questions or answers needed, just standing. We stood there for what felt like an eternity before a light appeared ahead. The water moved against the stones as it came closer. I breathed in, inhaling the sea air.

'Where are we?' I asked.

'The Bosphorus' he replied. 'Where east meets west.'

How ironic – the waterway met from different paths of life, as did we.

'Come' Onur ordered as the boat docked.

He held my hand and his grip felt reassuring. I followed his every step in my nude, strappy sandals. He pressed his hand on my lower back, ushering me to board the boat first. The group of women sat to our left stared. I wasn't sure if it was a look of jealousy or one of disapproval but I didn't care. Onur gestured towards the steps ahead, leading to the upper deck. I walked upwards, minding my step. The sandals weren't practical – no surprise there. Onur followed closely behind. Benches lined the deck and he gestured for me to sit. I took a seat and looked out to sea. There was nothing ahead, only lights twinkling in the distance and the gentle movement of the water below. The breeze blew across my face. Onur sat beside me, his body warming mine as he came close. His hand was on my leg once more, his lips edging toward mine. He kissed my neck. His gentle touch was something else, more than just lust.

'Why here?' he then asked.

'I don't know' I replied. It was the truth.

'I am happy you came' he said and to be honest, so was I.

I searched his face for something more. There was a faint scar above his brow, a few creases in his skin. I guessed he was older than I was. His facial hair was groomed, his brows trimmed. The open shirt exposed the ink shading his olive skin. Other than that, there was nothing more to read. I longed to know more of the man who seemed too perfect to be true.

'What does Onur mean?' I then asked.

'Honourable' he said. So far so good I thought.

He looked into my eyes once more. He was a man of few words. I couldn't help but wonder if he too had questions. Then again, maybe he was happy to only know my name. Perhaps this was a fleeting holiday romance, not a happily ever after. True as that may be, I wanted more. I couldn't cope with any more heartache. I pulled away.

'What's wrong?' he asked.

'Nothing' I replied, folding my arms to warm my bare skin.

I looked around, anywhere but into his gaze. There was an elderly couple sat directly opposite. Their skin was wrinkled, their posture frail. The creases marking their faces told the stories of their journey. Perhaps a truly remarkable one but an onlooker would never know. She looked content as she nestled close to her husband. Their withered hands held one another. The bands on their fingers declared their love. True love does last a lifetime I thought, admiring them. And how do we find true love if we run away from it? It's all about taking a chance. With that, I surrendered myself to the prospect of love, falling into Onur's embrace. He held me tightly once more. For love is not certain, it goes hand in hand with faith.

We sailed along the river.

'What would you like to know?' he asked, reading my mind.

'Anything' I said softly.

And so he began. 'I come from a poor family. My sister and I had nothing. I say to myself I want to change this fortune. That's why I am studying. One day, I will give my own children the life I never had.'

His emotions were clear across his face. There was determination in his voice. I smiled. It was warming to hear a part of his past, the hope of his future. And you can't fake emotion like that. It was enough, more than enough, for now anyway.

Music filled the silence. There was a stringed band on the decking, serenading all with their violins and cellos. Onur stood and held his hand out to take mine.

'Dance with me?' he then asked.

I'd never slow danced in my life. How very 1950's I thought. It seemed that dating and dirty dancing now went hand in hand – and nothing like Patrick Swayze that's for sure. Maybe it was more old-school here. Without further ado, I took his hand. He pulled me close and gently placed one hand on my lower back, the other caressing my palm. I placed mine on his shoulder and we swayed beneath the darkness. The silk of my dress blew against the breeze. The warmth of his touch pulsated through my body. I followed his every move. It was fairly simple and oh so romantic. I lost myself in the moment. He edged closer. He parted his lips slightly and kissed me. It wasn't lust – there was more to it than that. Perhaps fairy tales do exist after all.

It was late now. Our journey had come to an end. We were in a taxi once more, Onur's arms around me. I was happy, the happiest I'd been in a while. I could have sat there forever but the night had to end at some point. We pulled up outside the hotel and Onur stepped out first. I couldn't help but question if this was goodbye. Would I see him again? I wanted to ask him up but my head told me otherwise. He stepped towards me, our bodies inches apart.

'I had a lovely evening' I said, sincerely.

He smiled. No words were needed. I listened to my heart, reached for his hand and began to walk inside. He followed. It wasn't logic, it was fate.

Chapter Six

Here we were. I wondered what would happen next. Then again, we both knew. Onur closed the door to. I just stood there. He walked towards the desk and lifted the wilted rose petals with his fingers. He smiled and gazed towards me. I inhaled deeply. He edged closer. We were now standing inches apart. He grabbed my waist and pulled me in. His parted lips brushed against my ear and his hand skimmed across my breast. The silk of the dress grazed against my tender nipples. I leaned back, my mouth ajar as he slowly kissed my neck. I fell onto the bed, longing for his touch yet he just seemed to stare.

'You are beautiful Rose' he whispered. And this time I believed him.

He leaned forward, lifted the silk over my head and threw it to the floor. I lay there, naked upon the fresh cotton.

I blushed. I'd always thought I was far from perfect. Here I was, naked in front of a man I hardly knew and I'd never felt better. I felt alive. I brushed my hand across my bare breasts, caressing my hair with the other. I bit my lip. His gaze met mine. Onur slowly unbuttoned his shirt, revealing a toned canvas holding the stories of his journey. The inked words painted his torso. His muscles flexed as he dropped his jeans ever so slightly. I was mesmerised once more. He lowered his body to mine, holding our gaze. Then, he began to kiss my skin, grazing my nipples with his tongue. I arched my body to meet his, frustrated from the longing. I ran my fingers across his back. His mouth soon found mine, our lips locking. Then, he pulled back.

'*Sen benimsin*' he said. I had no idea what he had said but he spoke the words so tenderly.

He removed his jeans entirely, baring all. Now I knew why he was so smug. The weight of him on me, his bare skin moved against mine. I gripped the sheets, my back arching, the cotton rubbing against my skin. I lost myself in the moment. The passion was overpowering. Our bodies met time and time again. I became closer. We moved faster. I moaned at his touch, over and over. Then, our bodies stilled. Moments passed as we savoured the sensation. He held me tightly before falling beside me.

Wow. Granted, it had been a while but that was incredible. I can't say I'd had much experience. Samuel had no idea what he was doing. It was the first time for us both and well it wasn't great for me. It had lasted three minutes at best. And as for Mark, I'd always thought he was phenomenal. It couldn't get better than this though. Onur had aroused my very core. I lay on my back, breathing heavily. I glanced over at him, his skin glistening from our heated embrace. He was staring at me, smirking.

'Hi' he said.

I smiled, blushing ever so slightly. He then did something which was foreign to me. He pulled me close, wrapping his arms around my body, his legs entwining with mine. He inhaled deeply. It was strange. Mark had shown me nothing after sex. It was an emotionless act for him. Now I understood what true intimacy was.

'Do you do this often?' I winced as the words left my mouth.

'Sorry?' he questioned.

I couldn't bring myself to say it again. 'It doesn't matter' I replied, turning away.

'Say again' he asked.

How embarrassing. The moment was perfect and I had to open my big mouth.

'Do you do this often?' I asked again, my cheeks now crimson.

He laughed. I turned back and looked into his eyes. I felt foolish as he began to grin.

'Rose, I am thirty years old' he began. Thirty – I would have guessed twenty seven. 'I have been with many women, yes' he said.

I sighed. He was insanely gorgeous and charming. What was there not to love? I cast my eyes down, lifting the sheet to cover my breasts. I didn't feel quite like a fairy-tale princess right now. I was just another notch on his bedpost. He lifted my chin with his palm.

'None of them like you' he added.

He probably said the same thing to each girl he had wooed. Who was I kidding? Where could this even go? This time next week I would be living the ordinary life once more. I nestled into the nook and opened myself to the possibility of love, even if it may be a temporary romance. After all, I was happy.

It was early. The orange hue of the sunrise lit the room and a slight breeze blew through the open window. I pulled the sheets across my body, glancing to the left where Onur lay. He looked peaceful as he slept. I stared at him, admiring his inked torso. The words spanned across his chest, prints on his biceps. The detailing was exquisite. I tried to decipher any kind of meaning when his eyes opened. His irises were now a navy ocean.

'Good morning' he said, his voice was deep.

'Hi' I said softly.

'You are beautiful in this light' he said, always the charmer. 'I have to go' he then said.

'Oh' I replied, saddened.

I hadn't thought that he'd leave, not yet anyway. There we go. He'd had his way with me and that was that.

'But...' he began. I felt hope by the very word. 'This evening we will meet?' he asked.

I nodded. He leaned forward, kissing me tenderly before pressing his lips to my forehead. He headed towards the bathroom. I couldn't help but stare at his peachy bum, biting my lip in lust. He turned and winked.

I heard the faint dripping of water as he showered. Even though my body ached, I longed for more. It was a feeling like no other. I swung my legs around, my feet falling flat onto the carpet. I reached for my robe. The satin brushed against my tender nipples, cooling my skin ever so slightly. Coffee, I needed coffee. I headed over to the desk, smiling at the fallen rose petals which now lined it. I brushed my fingers across them, savouring the sentiment. I placed a cup under the espresso machine. I filled a second cup just in case he wanted some, placing his on the bedside table. I sat upon the cotton sheets and took a sip. That's exactly what I needed.

The bathroom door opened and steam filled the room. Onur stood in the doorway, a towel around his waist. His wet hair dripped upon his bare torso. I can't just stare. I looked down at the golden foam lining the coffee. Another look wouldn't hurt. It may be the last. I looked up once more, catching his gaze. Baring his teeth, he winked at me and I melted a little inside. He ruffled his hair with the towel and pulled on his jeans.

'I made you some coffee' I said, gesturing towards the cup on the nightstand.

He blew me a kiss and took a few sips. He looked at himself in the mirror. There was no doubt that he looked anything but handsome. He must have known this.

'I'll await tonight' he said, charmingly so.

He placed another kiss upon my lips and walked towards the door. He turned and winked once more, closing it behind him.

I fell back. It felt like a dream. It had all been surreal. I took another sip of coffee and it left a slight residue on the cup. I smiled, debating my fate. I looked out of the window and lost myself in the dreamy skies ahead.

Eve rang. It was a video call. She'd called last week and we had since texted. I smoothed down my post sex hair and answered.

'So you are alive?' she said sharply as the call connected.

I wanted to roll my eyes. She was like a big sister, always looking out for me.

'I've sent you messages but nothing. I rang your mum and she hasn't heard from you either. We've both been worried sick.'

I couldn't help but feel bad. I can only imagine that my mum was beside herself.

'I'm just happy to see you Ro' she then said, relaxing slightly. She'd called me Ro for as long as I could remember.

'I'm sorry. I've been busy and the internet has been a nightmare but I'm fine" I replied.

I never lied to Eve and what's more, I was more than fine.

'How are you?' I asked, before she could lecture me any longer.

'Well...' she began, rolling her eyes.

Eve spoke of how Susie, her little girl, had been teething for the past two weeks. She'd had a grand total of three hours sleep last night. I didn't envy that. Susie was an angel. She was eighteen months old with a few blonde curls and blue eyes. I'd babysat her a few times and she would always laugh mischievously but was good as gold. Eve then explained the argument she'd had with her husband about not mowing the lawn. Then, there was the childminder who had cancelled last minute and how she was beyond fed up with her job. I loved Eve but she had a tendency to overlook her perfect life.

'That's enough about me. I need more in my life than talk of dirty nappies and teething toddlers. Tell me about you' she said, her eyes widening.

'It's been fabulous' I began.

I spoke of the breathtaking sunsets, the enchanting views and exquisite food. We'd both studied Greek mythology and Roman architecture in college so I knew she'd appreciate the hidden gems in this city. She sighed in envy as she listened and it felt as though we were thirteen again, without a care in the world.

'Auntie Rose!' a little voice screamed.

Eve lifted Susie onto her lap and handed her the phone. I saw the inside of Susie's mouth, her dribble coating the camera. She babbled for a few minutes and we played peek-a-book – a game she'd always adored. She waved before running around the living room humming. She was a busy baby. Eve looked at her, love in her gaze. It was the same look as the one I'd seen the woman give her daughter yesterday.

'It sounds incredible Ro – so very dreamy. I can't wait to see you next week' she said.

Next week? It seemed too soon but truth be told, I had missed her.

'Shall we go for lunch next Tuesday?' I asked.

'Hell yes!' she replied. 'I can't remember the last time I socialised.'

'Perfect. You can pick a place' I said and she did a happy dance.

'Any other news?' she asked.

I was reluctant to speak of Onur. Eve despised Mark after the way he had treated me over the years and I didn't blame her. I'd spent countless nights crying on her sofa and she'd always considered his side. Well, that was until Sophie came onto the scene. That's the girl he cheated on me with – one of the girls anyway. Eve hated him after that and would sigh each and every time I'd go back to him. She was right all along. I knew what she'd say if I told her I'd met some handsome foreigner, yet alone if I told her we'd slept together. I blushed at the thought.

'Not really, no.' I replied. 'I've just been soaking up the culture.'

'Give me something Ro. I live vicariously through you, you know that' she said, turning back to check on Susie.

'I'll send you some photos' I said, humouring her.

'Please' she said. 'Ro, I'm going to have to go. I've got to get Susie to nursery. Promise me you'll text your mum?'

'I will do babe' I replied.

'Say goodbye to Auntie Rose' she said to Susie, pulling her up onto her lap. Susie waved frantically and Eve blew me a kiss.

I felt warm inside. I was lucky to have such a friend. I looked at my phone. There were three missed calls and nine text messages. I looked at the time. Mum would probably be at work already. She really did work too hard. I typed out a message and promised I'd call later. She'd look forward to that phone call all day. I sent a few photos to Eve and threw the phone down. I felt exhausted but I couldn't spend all day in bed. Onur had plans for tonight – whatever they may be. It couldn't get more romantic than dancing under the stars. I'd just have to wait and see. I needed a shower first. I brushed out the curls in my hair and stepped into the bathroom. I could faintly smell Onur's scent as I slipped off my robe. The hot water stung my body. I closed my eyes and pictured him.

I wiped the mirror with my palm and twisted my hair into a towel. The room was dim. I looked out of the window and dark clouds now covered the sky. The sun was absent but it was still hot. I sat on the bed and massaged lotion into my skin, easing the tension. The ruffled sheets made my body throb with desire.

Mum had replied. She had been worried. I was looking forward to catching up with her later. I wondered if I should mention Onur. Not yet, she'd only worry. And what was the point? Onur and I were nothing more than a fleeting romance. I sent her a few kisses back. I put on a cotton maxi dress and towel dried my hair before painting my lips peony. Now what? I couldn't spend the day here waiting for Onur. The weather wasn't great and I didn't feel like walking around another museum alone. I threw a few essentials into my tote and scrunched my damp hair.

'Good day Madam' said the concierge.

He was sweet. I smiled his way before stepping outside.

The rain drops were bouncing off the footpath. I waited underneath the canopy, debating which turn I should take.

'Taxi?' asked the doorman. I shook my head.

There were some shops at the end of street – perhaps I'd have a look. The stone building had green wooden shutters, the paint peeling. Glass jars filled with sweets lined the window. I'd always been more savoury than sweet but there wasn't any harm in looking. I stepped inside and an elderly gentleman welcomed me. It was magical. Rows of jars filled with boiled sweets of every colour. Cabinets were filled with pistachio coated dates and honey soaked figs. I stood in the midst of the shop, not knowing where to start. It was a little like *Charlie and the Chocolate Factory.* The gentleman gestured towards a display filled with *lokum*. He handed me a small piece of the jelly-like substance, coated with icing sugar. It was Turkish delight. I'd tried it before – in the form of Cadbury – but it was nothing like this. It was delicious. He handed me something else. It was sticky to touch. It was layers of pastry filled with what seemed to be pistachios and honey. It was super sweet but beautiful.

I must have been there for twenty minutes or so. I'd tried several flavours of Turkish delight and some roasted nuts. The shopkeeper was lovely. He didn't speak a word of English but he'd offered me some herbal tea to go with the sweet indulgcnccs. It would be rude not to buy something. I was the only one in the shop after all. I doubted he had many customers. Dad had always had a sweet tooth and I knew he'd love that honey soaked dessert – baklava. I pointed to it. The man began to place pieces into a small box and tied it with red ribbon. He bowed his head and I did the same and walked towards the door. Then, I stopped. I had a sudden thought.

Chapter Seven

The rain had stopped. I loved the smell after the rain. It was less humid now and the sky had cleared. I looked in the shop windows as I walked along the cobbles. There was a florist at end of this street. Terracotta pots were filled with bunches of lavender and jasmine and metal buckets held long-stem roses in every colour. I'd always loved the smell of fresh flowers. There was a plump lady sat on a wooden stool in the doorway. She nodded her head my way. She looked typically Turkish. She was wearing loose cotton clothes, a patterned headscarf and gold bangles on her wrists. I'd guess she was in her mid sixties.

'Hello' she then said.

'Hi' I replied, smiling.

'Is there something you are looking for?' she asked. She spoke English well. It was refreshing.

'No, nothing in particular' I said.

She leaned forward and picked up a crisp white rose. She held it to her nose and inhaled deeply.

'The most beautiful flower' she then said.

I'd always been a sucker for roses. Perhaps it was because of the rose bushes we had in our garden back home. Mum had always loved them, hence my name.

'Here we use rose for everything – perfumes, oils, jams and sweets' she continued.

She passed the rose to me and I breathed in the fragrance. She seemed like a kind soul. In this neighbourhood – the street name had slipped my mind – it was different. Traders seemed to have a passion for what they were selling. There was no shouting or haggling needed. It was outside of the tourist area. I picked a few single roses, a bunch of lavender and some fern. I handed the flowers to her to which she smiled and wrapped them in brown paper. I reached for my purse but she shook her head, implying that she didn't want payment. I frowned and handed her a few notes. Her worn clothes implied she was short of a penny or two.

'I insist' I said.

'Thank you my dear' she replied, smiling.

I walked away and the scent of lavender filled the air. The simplest of things are sometimes the most beautiful. She was prepared to give away her goods only to bring me happiness. I turned and smiled and she gave me a little wave.

Onur hadn't mentioned any details of our date. He was mysterious as ever. It was after three now and I had no idea when he'd come. I needed to look incredible. He'd caught me off guard twice – frizzing hair and all – but this time I knew he was coming. What to wear? Now that was the real question. I needed something that went with hunk. The backless satin would be a tad over the top and that nude slip was a little too revealing. I mentally pieced together outfits and vetoed each one. I then felt a drop of rain fall. It was early but I headed back to the hotel.

I fumbled in my bag for the room key, juggling my purchases. I was met once more with the smell of lavender and fresh cotton. It was like shopping at The White Company – crisp white bed linen, silks and displays of candles. The maid had folded my nightie and placed it across the pillow. There was a ceramic jug in the bathroom. I filled it with some cool water and arranged the fresh flowers. They smelt wonderful. I placed the brown paper bag from the sweet shop upon the desk. I had more than enough time so I dialled home.

'Rose! Hello my darling, how are you?'

'I'm good– well fabulous actually – I love it out here. And you would just love it too' I said as I went on to describe the magical city.

'Oh Rose, it sounds wonderful. I am so jealous' Mum replied.

I felt saddened by the fact that I'd gone without her. We had been inseparable since day one but I needed to do this on my own. She was forty six but looked at least ten years younger with her bouncy curls and toned figure. She was a sucker for yoga and it really showed. People had always assumed that we were sisters – something she just loved to hear. She was a lawyer but always dreamed of retiring to a little Italian village by the coast. She had a designer lifestyle but she'd change it all for a simple life sampling local wine and cheeses in the sun. I just hoped that her dream would one day become a reality as she really did deserve nothing but happiness. She told me about how stressed she was at work – nothing new there – and how she'd joined a new meditation class. I honestly didn't know how she found the time. She then went on tell me how she had bickered with Dad about decorating the house.

'We've had that ugly wallpaper in the hallway for years so I suggested that we simply strip the walls and paint them an off-grey – dusted cappuccino as it were. Well, your father went on to lecture me that the wallpaper hid the cracks in the wall to which I said that the cracks added character to the property. He didn't agree with that either so we had a tiff' she explained.

'So what did you decide on then?' I asked.

'Well your father apologised and he's just been to pick up the paint. I do hope that this dusted cappuccino isn't too dark.'

I adored my parents. My father was a humble man. He enjoyed the simplicities of life – watching a light-hearted black and white film on a rainy afternoon was his calm. It was easier for him to agree to avoid an argument at times. Well, they never really argued, just bickered. They had been married for twenty seven years now and what a wonderful marriage they had had. High school sweethearts, they'd lived on the same road and played in the street together since as far back as they can remember. They courted – as they put it – throughout high school, sending each other love notes in class. They were in their late teens when my dad proposed and they were wed the following year. It is my grandma who tells me the stories. The wedding was held in a beautiful little church and my mum wore an ivory dress and carried a bouquet of lemon coloured roses. She would share the details of my parents' lives before they had me and I would sit and loose myself in the wonderful tales. True love can last a lifetime it seems.

'How is Dad?' I asked.

'He's good sweetheart. Well, you know your father, he's been pottering around the house, keeping himself busy. He misses you.'

It was true they idolised me. I'd lived at home even whilst at university. I'd always been a home bird and I couldn't bring myself to live in some grotty student house. Beth – a girl on my course – had mould growing in her bath tub and rats in her kitchen. Not for me. This was the first time I'd been away from home for more than a few days. She called my dad.

'Hey titch' he said, coming into view.

He had called me titch for as long as I could remember. It just stuck and would feel strange now if he didn't. He had greying stubble and laughter lines painted his face. His hugs were the best – bear hugs as I called them. He was a loveable soul. He was in the garden watering a new plant. I shared a couple of stories before he lectured me on keeping my valuables close at all times.

'Rose, make sure that you keep your bag close to you. Don't put it down, even for a second' he said.

'Okay' I replied, rolling my eyes. I noted that I did this a lot.

'And your passport, where is that? Do you have a safe at the hotel?' His questions were endless.

It was warming that he had always cared for me so.

'I love you titch. Please take care' he said passing the phone back to my mum. She was dying to speak some more.

She walked back inside. 'Have you met anyone?' she asked, lowering her voice, her eyes widening.

I desperately wanted to share the details of my whirlwind romance with someone but now wasn't the time. She'd only worry, just like she had done when I was with Mark. I'd find another time to tell her, the right time.

'No, no one' I replied. I hated lying to her.

She sighed a little and we went on talking for some time. It was like a breath of fresh air.

It was almost five now. I let my clothes drop to the floor and stepped in the shower. The hot water beat against my back, washing away the dirt of the city. I hummed a little, eager to see my man of the moment once more.

It was dusk, just past eight. I was ready and damn I looked good. I rarely said that about myself but I felt fabulous. I brushed another stroke of red across my lips. The glossy curls in my hair bounced with each step. I was wearing a velvet crimson dress and black satin courts. I'd tried on several outfits but this dress had something about it. I'd got it at a sample sale on Oxford Street – a bargain. Not quite a steal but a third of the designer price tag. I'd just about managed to fasten the zip – it was no secret that I'd gained a few pounds. I popped the lipstick back inside my clutch. Now what? I perched on the edge of the bed, careful not to mess my look and waited. The gentle patter of rain fell against the windowpane as I watched the time tick by.

Nine thirty. He's not coming. I looked down, feeling foolish. I was my sixteen year old self once more. Samuel had promised me the world but he'd never called after we'd had sex all those years ago. This was the same story. There had been no phone numbers or surnames exchanged. Onur knew what he was doing. I couldn't believe it. He seemed different and I told myself he'd show. I wanted to believe he would. I dabbed a little Chanel across my wrists and behind my ear. Each time I heard footsteps I stilled but they would always carry on down the corridor. I glanced around the room. The petals of the rose had wilted a little in the heat and in that moment everything seemed so different. The light was dim, the rose dead. I fell amongst the feathered pillows, no longer concerned about my looks. I closed my eyes tightly to stop the tears. Why had I fallen into the same trap yet again?

I stirred. There was a dull thud. I opened my eyes, my head hazy. Had I slept? I looked down to see that I was still fully dressed. Oh yes, I'd been stood up. There it was again. I smoothed my hair and brushed the velvet of my dress. I hoped it was him. I stood, taking my time. He'd have to wait. It was late and he knew I'd be waiting. Mark had always been the same. He was always late for date night – another business meeting or something or other. He'd come when he was ready and loved having that power over me. My lipstick had smudged a little. I painted my lips with red once more and sprayed myself with Chanel. I took a deep breath and opened the door ever so slightly. And there he was. I opened the door fully and his expression dropped, his eyes widening.

'Wow' he mouthed. His mouth was ajar.

I had to admit, I was a little smug. I guess it made a change from it always being him.

'You are beautiful' he said. I blushed.

He was wearing a pair of grey, slim-fit trousers with a brown leather shoe and a black shirt which was unbuttoned slightly – true to form. His stubble was thicker now.

'It's late' I said.

'The night has only just begun' he replied.

I refrained from rolling my eyes, as per usual.

'Come in?' I asked.

I longed for him to say yes as I pictured our last heated embrace. He leaned against the wall, edging closer.

'Come with me' he said, holding his hand out for mine.

He was taxing. I felt my body pulse with frustration. I reached for his hand and his touch sent a shiver through my body. I looked timidly into his eyes. Hand in hand, we walked down the hallway. It wasn't until we reached the elevator that he spoke.

'How was your day?' he asked. It was different. He seemed interested.

'It's been okay.' I replied. I did a little shopping and spoke to my parents.'

His face seemed to light up. 'Your parents, what are they like?' he then asked.

I spoke about them briefly as we made our way down to reception. He would nod and smile as I explained their personalities and details of our home life. I was just about to ask about his family but was distracted by the way people were looking at us. The concierge shot us a disapproving look whilst guests in the lobby whispered and stared. What on earth? I looked down, checking my appearance. Nothing said hooker about this outfit – not to me anyway.

The rain had thankfully stopped. I began to walk over to a taxi which was parked on the curb. The driver

smiled and opened the door but Onur pulled me back. I
turned and looked at him, frowning.

'We can walk' he said, his eyes smiling.

'Oh, okay' I replied, nodding to the driver in
apology.

He reached for my hand and we walked side by side
through the cobbled streets. We shared a few words and
exchanged glances until we made another left turn. Then he
stopped.

'Here we go' he said.

My face dropped. It was a dark, narrow alleyway.
The only thing in view was a kebab stall. You have to be
kidding me? I gazed down at my dress.

'You're joking?' I finally managed, raising my
brows.

He smirked a little. 'Trust me.'

Onur walked over to the stall. I had to admit, the
smell was something else. My stomach growled as I inhaled
the spiced notes in the air. I gazed up. Nothing but
moonlight and a dim oil lamp lit the cobbles ahead. A warm
breeze blew across the street. I glanced back at Onur and
couldn't believe what I was seeing. The man had pulled
three plastic stools out from behind his stall. Onur had
placed a white napkin across one. He then pulled a tea light
from his pocket – our centrepiece as it seemed – lighting it
and gestured for me to sit. I couldn't help but laugh. I sat,
careful that I didn't snag my dress on the rough plastic.
Onur sat too. The man began grilling vegetables and slicing

the meat with the largest knife I'd ever seen. Onur reached for my hand across our so-called table. I wasn't a snob in any respect but I wasn't used to this. I loved street food. There was always a new market popping up in the middle of London and the food to go was delicious. Never had I eaten a Greek gyro in an evening dress though. I suppose there's no harm trying something new from time to time. Mark had always taken me to five star restaurants in Chelsea with a bottle of champagne awaiting us. It was all about status and money and well this was humble.

The man placed the food down in front of us. It was served on paper plates with a plastic fork. Onur spoke to the man, thanking him as it seemed. I was still in awe of the language. I was clueless but it was fascinating nonetheless.

'How you say...' began Onur. 'Onc moment' he said, scrolling through his phone. 'Bon appétit is it?' he asked. His pronunciation was slightly off but after all, it was French.

'How do you say that in Turkish?' I asked.

'*Afiyet olsun*' he replied.

I repeated the words and he smiled infectiously back at me.

Oh my. The lamb melted on my tongue, the spices lingering afterwards. It was beyond tender. The vegetables were seasoned to perfection and the yogurt and mint dip complimented everything in sight. I'd catcn at some fairly incredible restaurants in my time but this was out of this world.

'Good?' asked Onur.

'It's delicious!' I exclaimed, indulging in another forkful.

I nodded my head in gratitude to the man as he cleared away our plates. He threw them straight in the bin – no washing up. A truly wonderful cook, lost in some alleyway of a vast city. It was a shame to hide such talent but he seemed happy enough. Photographs of what appeared to be his love ones were pinned to his stall.

I was full. I hadn't bargained for eating so much but it would have been rude not to. Onur reached for a glass jar on the side and poured a little of the liquid into his hands, rubbing them together. The scent of lemon filled the air.

'Let's go' he said as he took my hand.

I grabbed my clutch and held his hand tightly.

'You continue to surprise me' I said as we walked through the streets.

'Why?' he asked, frowning.

'I thought we would dine in a restaurant, not on the street' I said.

His face dropped, searching mine.

'I loved it' I then exclaimed.

He put his arm around my shoulders and held me close as we walked. I felt safe. I felt content.

'Fancy a drink?' he asked as we stopped outside a bar.

A drink – yes I needed a drink. I wasn't sure why but my nerves were shot when I was around him. I nodded in response.

There were cushions placed amongst wooden tables which were low to the floor. Lanterns, like the one Onur had bought for me, hung from the ceiling. Onur gestured towards a table and I sat as gracefully as possible. I neatened the velvet of the dress to cover my knees, placing my legs to the side and leaned into Onur's embrace. He loosened another button on his shirt, revealing yet another story. I nestled close and noticed something I hadn't before. A faint scar painted across his chest. The scar was thick, twisted in places, hidden amongst the foreign words on his torso. I couldn't help but wonder how it had happened. Had it been an accident or perhaps a war wound? It was a story for another day. This was just a fleeting romance after all.

Onur gazed around the room and I nestled into him. The waiter asked Onur a question – presumably what we wanted. His eyes never met mine. He had ordered for me. I'd always hated it when Mark would do so. It was as if he knew best.

'What did you order?' I asked, curtly.

'Wait and see' Onur replied.

'But how did you know what I wanted?'

'Trust me, you'll like' he said, smirking.

There it was again, his smugness. He held a twinkle in his eye. It was hard not to smile at his charm. I leaned into him and he held me closely.

The waiter carried a brass tray which held two straight glasses filled with a white substance. I frowned, wondering what it may be. Onur thanked him as he placed the glasses upon the wood and he handed one to me.

'Lion's milk' he then said.

'Excuse me?' I asked – lost in the translation perhaps?

Onur laughed. 'It's *rakı* but we Turks call it lion's milk' he then clarified. 'They say that men who drink this are strong.' He winked.

I laughed. You learn something new each day I guess.

We chinked our glasses together and I took a sip. It tasted exactly like sambuca. I'd never been a huge fan of spirits. When I'd turned eighteen, I was dared to down eighteen shots of tequila by the hot bartender – a bad move to say the least. I couldn't even tell you how many I'd managed. I woke up naked in the bath with absolutely no recollection of the rest of the night. I winced at the thought and had vowed never to drink tequila again. I took another sip. It was diluted with water and was actually quite nice.

The waiter was back once more. This time he placed a water pipe on the floor. It took me back to the days of reading *Alice in Wonderland* where the caterpillar puffed away upon the mushroom. It was a time when everything was innocent. Onur inhaled deeply and then exhaled the smoke. The clouds lingered across the room. He passed it to me and I shook my head. He breathed in once more, this time blowing circles of smoke up into the air. How did he do that? He winked. The pipe itself was beautiful. The gold leaf pattern swirled amongst emerald greens. I took another sip of the lion's milk and I felt a little tipsy. I wasn't sure if it was from the smoke or the drink. I breathed in the smoke which filled the room. It was surprisingly sweet.

'It is not tobacco' Onur said, as though reading my thoughts. 'It is strawberry.'

I took the pipe from his grip and inhaled. It caught the back of my throat. I tried not to cough as I blew the smoke out. Granted, it wasn't bad at all. I took another puff and passed it back to him.

We had hardly spoken since sitting here – nothing new. I looked at Onur. His stubble was slightly shorter today, creases coated his forehead and his usual smell of vanilla and tobacco seemed stronger than ever this evening. I scanned the room. There were three men sat across from us, all sporting dark beards. They were the only other people in the bar, besides a handful of waiters. I locked the gaze of one of the men. How embarrassing. I lowered my head. I smoothed the velvet of my dress before looking up once more. He was still looking at me. And then he smiled. I looked down and twisted the ends of my hair before I looked at Onur. It was clear that he'd clocked the guy. He was staring directly at him. His body seemed rigid, his breathing shallow. He had since placed the pipe down upon the table and his hand formed into a fist. Oh god. I held my breath.

Chapter Eight

Onur's eyes held a green glare. It was the look of jealousy. The man was still staring my way. It was a triangle of gazes which didn't seem likely to end well.

'Let's go' I said.

He didn't reply. I stroked his arm to calm him but his body tensed all the more. The skin was stretched across his knuckles as it held a fist. The guy wasn't even my type – nothing like Onur. He had a big frame, chubby around the edges, very short hair and a beard which was anything but groomed. Then, he winked at me.

It all happened so fast. Onur flew towards him, his clenched fist striking his face. The man fell backwards and hit his head on the wall behind. His nose bled, red staining his linen shirt. The others stood. It was two against one now. The music became inaudible against the raised voices and the waiters watched from afar. It must have been a regular occurrence as they didn't seem fazed whatsoever. They seemed to be wagering who would win. Onur pressed his face against one of the others' and spoke through gritted teeth. I'd seen fights – if that's what you could call them – in London but nothing like this. This was a brawl. I just sat there, spellbound.

I couldn't help but think it was my fault. I'd looked his way. Onur and the others were still shouting whilst the other man rocked back and forth on the floor, blood running down his face. This was not the fairy-tale ending I'd wished for. I stood, stepped into my shoes and made my way towards the door. He didn't see me leave.

I walked slowly down the cobbled street. Everything had seemed so perfect – perhaps a little too perfect. I guess we had to come back down to earth at some stage. The air was cooler now. I hugged my bare skin as I walked. I had no idea where I was heading but parts looked familiar. The hotel surely couldn't be too far. People stared as I passed. The locals muttered amongst themselves. I felt anything but special, very foolish actually.

I came to a crossway. I pondered which way to turn, making a left ahead. Then, a hand grabbed my wrist, pulling me backwards. I gasped and spun around. It was Mr. Tall, Dark and Handsome. His complexion was calmer, his touch softer. I held his gaze, his irises a cool blue once more.

'Rose' he whispered.

I turned on my heel. I had nothing to say to him.

'Rose' he said again, more sternly.

I took another step forward. This time he grabbed my waist, pulling me into him. I tried to free myself from his touch. I struggled against him. He held me tighter. He lifted my chin, heightening my lips to reach his.

'Remember, you are mine' he spoke, his lips now parted.

The smell of smoke on his breath was stronger than ever. The alcohol stung as he pressed his lips to mine. I wanted to run. Instead, I fell deeper than ever into his embrace. I lost all self control. I couldn't move as he held me tightly. But, I didn't want to. I was under his spell once again.

'Sorry' I sighed. The words were barely inaudible but he heard nonetheless.

'Sorry?' he questioned, frowning.

I looked at my feet. 'That was my fault' I replied.

Onur inhaled deeply. The situation was obviously still raw.

'Listen' he said calmly. 'All you need to be is mine.'

Be his? Was it really that simple? It seemed complicated and I didn't want complicated at this point in my life.

'Be mine?' he asked, again.

Our whirlwind romance flashed in front of me – our dreamy dance under the stars, the out-of-this-world sex, and the rose. Everything had been magical until now. That side of him in the bar, the guy who likes a fist fight, well that was anything but magical.

'Be mine?' he said softly.

And for the first time he seemed anything but sure of himself. He too was unsure of my answer. His eyes were full of hope. I paused as he held his breath, awaiting my reply.

'We will have to wait and see' I said, winking at him.

'I'll take that for now' he replied, smiling. He took my hand and we strolled through the streets.

It wasn't long before we were outside the hotel again.

'Do you want to come up?' I asked, hopefully.

'What do you think?' he said. The smugness was back.

Hand in hand, we walked through reception. People were still staring. This time, I didn't care. Onur pressed his hand against the nape of my back, ushering me into the lift. We rode in silence. I longed for his touch, dreaming of the incredible sex.

I half expected Onur to throw me onto the bed and ravish me to an inch of my life as we entered the room. Instead, he sat at the desk, staring as I slid off my shoes.

'What?' I asked shyly.

'Nothing' he said.

I desperately wanted to ask him about the fight and why he had started it. We could have left and avoided it all. I sat on the edge of the bed, pressing my feet into the carpet.

'What is Rose thinking?' he then asked. It must have been clear that something was bothering me.

'I was thinking...' I paused for a second. 'Actually, it doesn't matter.'

'No, say' he said.

'What just happened?'

It was like ripping off a plaster. Onur inhaled deeply and looked up at the ceiling. His expression changed.

'I just don't understand. That man was only looking at me and then, well everything else was a blur. Do you like to fight?' I asked.

'Rose' he began. I still loved the way he curled his tongue around my name. 'It is hard to say. I am a jealous man. That man, he was looking at you. He wants you. I saw this and I don't like. I am with you, not him. You are mine, not his. I don't know what men are like where you come from but here we fight for what is ours. No, I don't like to fight. I never liked it. Sometimes in this life you have to do things you don't like. I feel something tonight, something I did not feel before. I feel something for you.'

I think it was the most I'd heard him say. Mark had never declared his love for me but here was a man, a man I hardly knew, saying all the right things. He felt something for me. Perhaps it wasn't a fleeting romance after all. This drop-dead-gorgeous man wanted me to be his.

'You need time, yes?' he asked. I nodded. 'I can wait for you but I hope that you're answer is the right one.'

I stood and walked to the desk where he was sitting. I sat upon his knee and nested myself into him, inhaling his scent. I rolled my finger across his chest, across the scar. Could it be the mark from a brawl over another lover? He caressed my hair, his touch warming. I looked at his hand, red and swollen.

'Does it hurt?' I asked.

He shook his head but I kissed it better anyway.

'When will you leave?' he then asked.

I hadn't thought about leaving but this was in fact my fourth day here. 'I leave in three days' I answered.

There was now a cloud over us. We were silent.

'I have to go home in the next few days. My cousin is getting married' he said.

What? That's it? This romance certainly was fleeting.

He paused. 'Will you come with me?' he then asked.

I was taken aback. I hadn't bargained for this. I was dreading going back to the ordinary life in ordinary England but stay longer? Was he serious? I'd love to see his home – wherever that may be – but was this really a good idea?

'I'm not sure' I replied.

'Will you think about it?' he asked, hope in his voice.

I nodded and he squeezed me tightly. There were many promises to be made. We sat in each others' arms for what felt like an eternity. I snuggled into the nook, dreaming of coastal sunsets and orange groves.

I wasn't sure if I had drifted in and out of sleep. My head felt dizzy. We were still in the same position. I could spend all day in his arms. I glanced up. Onur was awake, looking down at me. I smiled.

'Hi' I murmured.

I was a little stiff. I don't know how long we had been sat there. I moved, stretching my legs out. Onur placed his hand under my bottom and flung my arms around his neck. Picking me up, he carried me to the bed. I longed for him. As he placed me down, he kissed my forehead and ran his hand over my face.

'Sleep, my dear Rose' he said.

Sleep? What happened to the out-of-this-world sex?

I sat up. 'Are you going to stay?' I asked. Gosh, I sounded desperate.

'If you want me to?' he questioned.

'I'd love it if you did' I answered, softly.

Onur smiled. He unbuttoned his shirt, placing it across the chair. He was handsome but that body was a bonus. I bit my lip as I watched him undress. He placed his things meticulously upon the desk, in line with the brown paper bag.

'That's for you' I then said.

Onur looked my way, frowning.

'That' I said again, gesturing towards the bag on the desk.

He carefully picked it up, peeling back the paper. 'Turkish delight?' he asked.

'Yes but what flavour is it?'

He smiled. It was a different smile – one not of lust but one of love.

'Rose – your favourite flavour' I then said.

He laughed. He came towards me and kissed my cheek tenderly. '*Gülüm*' he said. And I guess I was his after all.

He popped a piece in his mouth, the icing sugar coating his beard.

'Well?' I asked.

Onur closed his eyes, savouring the taste.

'Sweet like you' he finally replied.

He picked up another piece and held it towards my lips. I opened my mouth, licking the icing sugar off his finger as he placed it on my tongue. To be fair, it was delicious – and so was the Turkish delight.

Chapter Nine

The next day was a bit of a blur. I'd spent the night mulling over his proposal. I would convince myself to take a chance but then I'd soon think how silly the idea was. We both knew this had no future. And what's more, what would people think? Rose fell in love with some hot foreigner. There would be scandalous rumours I'm sure. I shouldn't go. I looked at Onur – gosh he was dreamy – and I was back at square one again. It would only be a week or so more. What harm would it be?

Onur stirred. I nestled myself into his arms. He kissed my forehead, his eyes sleepy.

'Good morning' I said softly.

He murmured, holding me tightly. I felt love drunk – tipsy over the man who lay beside me. And I couldn't quite put my finger on it but somehow it just felt right.

'I've been thinking' I began. I gave myself a second to muse one last time.

Onur propped himself up with one arm, holding my body with the other. He moved the silk of my nightie across my thigh. Holding my gaze, he listened intently. This was new to me. I'd always had to fight for Mark's attention. He would be busy with work, answering business calls in the middle of our date. I hated it but it had become the norm. Onur, on the other hand, clung to my every word as if mesmerised. I lost myself in his eyes and, without another thought, I had my answer.

'I'd love to see your home. That's if you'll still have me?'

Now that's what I call out-of-this-world sex. Onur was over the moon. It felt right – like it was meant to be or something. I couldn't quite explain it. We walked through the cobbled streets a few hours later. I had many thoughts. I'd need to tell love ones back home that I wouldn't be there this weekend as planned. They'd be disappointed but this was my life. I rehearsed what I'd say. *I've met this tall, dark and handsome stranger who wants me to be his. He's taking me to meet his family and live happily ever after*, humming the sound of church bells – maybe not. They would worry, that's a given, but at least I was happy. Now a skip in my step, I swung our linked hands back and forth. Onur walked silently beside me. It felt like we were young and in love without a care in the world – just as it should be.

The next few days passed. I still couldn't believe that I was staying here, well for another week anyway. Onur and I had been inseparable since that night. More wonderful memories and it hadn't even been a week since we'd met. We had taken a walk, shaded beneath the trees. There was a dinner date – nothing fancy yet wonderful. And who could forget the nights. I longed for our bodies to meet again. The week had been an everlasting moment of passion.

'Rose' he spoke, interrupting my thoughts.

'Yes' I replied softly.

'What is being your answer?' he then asked.

I frowned. I'd already said yes. I'd changed my flight – well actually I'd left it open.

'Yes' I said, a little confused.

'No' he then said. 'You misunderstand. What is your answer? Will you be mine?'

'I told you, you will have to wait and see' I replied, unsure of how he would respond.

Onur sighed and turned his body away from mine.

'Hey' I said, softly touching his shoulder.

I'd bruised his male ego. I desperately wanted to be his, who wouldn't? I just couldn't go through the heartache again. I'd thought Mark was the love of my life but that sparkle soon faded and reality hit. I had been nothing more than another notch on his bedpost. I lay on my back, staring at the ceiling. And then I spoke the truth.

'I was hurt and I still hurt now. I can't bear to go through that again.'

I stared at the white washed ceiling, expressionless. Onur turned to look at my blank face.

'Rose, I will never hurt you. Do you hear me? I will never hurt you.'

He said the words with such emotion. It was a promise and I couldn't help but believe him. I snuggled into his embrace and felt safe in his arms.

Onur ran a few errands the following morning before we left for his hometown. I'd been putting it off but I needed to let the rest of the world – my little world – know of my plans. I should have told them sooner but I didn't want the bubble bursting. I took and a deep breath and dialled home.

'Hi sweetheart' she said, joyfully. Oh how I loved her voice.

'Hi Mum, how're you?' I said.

'I'm fabulous darling. I've just picked up an oak unit for the hallway. It's coming together now. I can't wait for you to see it. I must have been an interior designer in another life you know. The ideas just come to me. I can't say the same for your dad though. He said we should paint the hallway red. He doesn't have a clue. Anyway, how're you sweetheart? All packed and ready for home? I can't wait to see you, I've missed my girl. Just remind me what time your-'

'I've got something to tell you' I said, cutting her off mid sentence.

Her tone changed in an instant. 'What's wrong?' she asked. Her voice was tense.

'I've kind of met someone and I've, well, I've decided to stay here a little longer.' I bit my lip, awaiting her reply.

'Oh. Well that is a surprise. Who is he?' she asked.

'His name is Onur and he's just dreamy. Besides, you were the one said I should meet someone and that's exactly what I've done. I couldn't be happier.'

There were a hundred questions to be asked but she just remained silent. I knew that she would worry. I rolled my eyes a little as I waited for her to respond.

'I'm happy for you sweetheart. You know me, I just worry. How long will you stay?'

'Only a week longer but please don't worry, I am living the dream' I replied.

'As long as you're happy then that's all that matters my love. How exciting. What's he like?' She lowered her voice 'Tell me everything.'

I lost myself in the tales of our love story as I narrated the events of this past week. She said how he sounded like a romantic at heart and a true gentleman – he was. She was a little upset that I hadn't confided in her sooner. Like she said *we tell each other everything,* which was true. I asked her not to mention it to Dad and she said she'd come up with something believable to tell him. He'd only worry if he knew I was in love with a handsome foreigner. I told her not to worry for the millionth time and then rang Eve. I couldn't wait to share every detail with her.

'Hey you' she said, her face a little blurry.

I could hear Susie singing in the background.

'How're you babe?' I asked.

'Tired, I am so tired. Susie is sleeping in our bed every night. I know, I know, I shouldn't let her but how can I say no to her little face? H isn't happy as we haven't had sex in weeks or it might even be months now, I've lost track. Nothing else is new, boring as per usual. What about you Ro? I'll be seeing you this time tomorrow!'

Oh great, I didn't want to tell her.

'What is it?' she then asked when I didn't respond.

'I've kind of met someone' I said, a little sheepishly.

'What?' she exclaimed.

'I've met someone here but honestly, I've never felt like this before and well, he's asked me to stay here with him for another week and I'm going to.'

There was silence, well apart from Susie babbling to her teddy bear.

'Eve?'

'Ro, I just don't know' she finally said. 'You said the same thing about Mark when you first met him. You thought it was all roses but the thorns tore you apart in the end. I just worry. I mean, I don't want to see you in a mess like before. What's this guy like?'

I went on to share the details of the past week, reliving it once more.

'He sounds like a dream, he really does. Please promise me you'll be careful? I just worry that it'll fall apart and you'll be right back to where you started. This trip was supposed to be for you, to find yourself. I want you to be happy Ro, more than anything, I really do. I just think it's all a bit fast, don't you?'

'I promise I'll be more careful this time.' I said. That was true. I didn't want a broken heart a second time.

'We love you lots' said Eve. Susie screamed *love you* in the background. She was an angel. 'Oh, I almost forgot, have you, well you know? she said quietly, her eyes widening.

'You could put it that way' I replied, smugly.

'And?' she asked, impatiently.

'Let's just say it was sweet, like Turkish delight.'

We both laughed. I blew a kiss to Eve and one for Susie and ended the call.

It was dusk before I knew it. We were due to leave in an hour or so and I wasn't yet dressed. I'd spent the day packing my things and I couldn't be happier that the journey wasn't over. I dreamed of what would come next. The call to prayer sounded. I leaned out of the Juliette balcony, admiring all in sight. It was beautiful. An orange hue lit the sky overhead. The smell of jasmine lingered in the air. Now this is living.

It wasn't long before there was a slight knock at the door. It was him, my love. I'd since showered, tied my hair into a loose chignon and slipped into a satin navy jumpsuit. I ran a shade of peony across my lips and misted my neck with Chanel. Truth be told, it was a little over the top as we were travelling through the night. The door ajar, Onur bent slightly to kiss my forehead with nothing but affection. He was wearing linen trousers and a navy cotton shirt. He was handsome as always. He smiled and his eyes sparkled against the subdued light.

'Ready?' he asked.

I nodded my head and he took my suitcase from me. I scanned the room, making sure that I'd got everything. I turned, glancing at the fallen rose petals. How things had changed in a week. I closed the door softly, leaving what felt like the past behind and taking a leap of faith to see what could be my future. Only you hold the key to writing your own wonderful story.

Chapter Ten

We had only been on the bus for the best part of thirty minutes and I was fed up. The seats were anything but comfortable. They were lumpy and smelt stale. There was no leg room whatsoever, the air-con was broken and everything in sight was sticky. Let's just say that we weren't travelling in style. The bus would rock back and forth each time we stopped at a red light. It took me back to nights at the fair. The sickly smell of doughnuts and candyfloss mixed with a ride on the teacups. I took a deep breath and looked around. I'd guess that most, if not all, of the passengers were Turkish. Perhaps they too were making their way home. There was a screaming toddler opposite which didn't help my mood. He repeatedly banged his plastic toys against the window and babbled away. Onur was sound asleep. His legs stretched out into the aisle. I sat there, more awake than ever as I flicked through a copy of last month's *Vogue*. It was one I'd read at least three times already.

Two hours had passed. Onur was still asleep. He hadn't even moved and looked peaceful as ever. I, on the other hand, became more annoyed with each jolting motion. I'd chomped my way through half a pack of biscuits from the tuck shop – nothing like a chocolate digestive or better still a bourbon – and read *Vogue* twice over. It was pitch black outside and the driver had since dimmed the lights. Now would be the perfect time to see what was happening in the world. I'd love to see what hot gossip was splashed across social media. Rose, live for the moment I told myself. Well this certainly wasn't a moment which I'd want to relive any time soon that's for sure. The thought of scandalous news faded and I closed my eyes, pleading to sleep. I fidgeted in hope that Onur would wake. He stirred. I coughed loudly and he opened his eyes.

'You okay?' he asked.

I shrugged. It's funny, I'd wanted him to wake up for hours, quite literally, but now that he was awake it only made me even more irritable. He closed his eyes again as I ignored his question.

'How long have we got left?' I finally asked.

He stretched before squinting at his watch. 'Eight hours or so' he muttered.

'Eight hours?' I shrieked.

You have to be kidding me? He'd said it was a long trip but come on. I hadn't bargained for a ten hour journey on this hell hole. I rolled my eyes and looked up at the ceiling.

'Come here' he said.

He pulled me into the nook and stroked my arm. It was too hot but I couldn't say no. I leaned into him and exhaled.

'It'll be worth it. Wait and see' he said.

Oh it better be I thought.

The bus jolted and my neck lunged backwards. I looked around, a little disorientated. I must have slept. I glanced at the hands of Onur's watch with great difficulty as he slept. Triple checking I was reading it right – it is hard upside down and in the dark – it seemed that I'd been asleep for almost three hours. It's like that moment on the plane when you feel like you've slept for an eternity yet it has only been through take off – twenty minutes at best. Luckily, and for my own sanity, it wasn't like that today. I stretched as best I could and sipped a little water. I felt sticky. My jumpsuit was creased beyond belief. I rummaged in my bag for a mirror – flat hair, smudged lipstick and a pale and dry complexion. I misted myself with some facial spray and scrunched my hair with coconut oil. I looked outside. It was hard to see anything in this light. Every street looked the same as the last. I could make out a few buildings but nothing more. The bus jolted yet again. It was a good job I wasn't a queasy traveller. I couldn't say the same for the gentleman at the back from the sounds of things.

It wasn't long before we stopped. I nudged Onur. His eyes were sleepy but he managed to smile my way. The driver began speaking and it wasn't long before everyone stood, collecting their belongings and making their way to the front of the bus.

'What's happening?' I asked, praying that we hadn't broken down. I honestly don't think I could cope if we had.

'We are staying here tonight' Onur replied.

'Oh' I said.

I wasn't sure if I was happy or not. I'd be glad to get off this bus but I'd rather keep going. The sooner this journey came to an end, the better.

'It'll be fun' Onur said, reading my mind.

Everyone clambered off the bus. We'd parked in front of a hotel – a lovely hotel in truth. Perhaps this was the silver lining after all. I imagined it to be like the horrors of Brontë's *Wuthering Heights*. What lay in front of us was a stone building adorned with pretty flowers and fountains lining the front entrance. It was quaint but aren't those the best type of places? The driver led us into the foyer and each couple checked in one after the other. The little boy was now a dead weight over his dad's shoulder in front. It wasn't long before it was our turn. The receptionist spoke to Onur first before turning to me.

'Madam, please may I see your passport?' he asked.

I nodded, fumbling in my bag. I handed it to him and he thanked me.

He typed our details into his computer, smiling away. He seemed to be quite a happy chap saying it was now past midnight. He frowned and then asked Onur something. Onur replied without hesitation and the receptionist chuckled.

'Congratulations' he said to me with a huge grin.

I gave him an awkward smile. I was clueless.

'I'll be sure to send something special to your room. You are in fact the second couple this week to get engaged.'

Engaged?! Wait what? Had I missed something? I shot Onur a look but he looked ahead. The man handed us our keys, winking before beckoning the next couple.

I was stunned. I was unable to speak. It wasn't until we were in the lift that I could string words together.

'Engaged?' I yelled.

Onur laughed. 'It is, how you say, not respectful to sleep together. We are not married and this, well it brings a lot of questions. He asked if we were married so I said I'd just proposed.'

I suppose it made sense but I felt like wedding bells had passed me by quicker than you could say *I do*. And what's more, he didn't seem to think this was a big deal. He seemed to shrug it off like he'd done this several times before. What's worse is that he probably had. I could stay mad or I could laugh and enjoy the evening. I opted for the latter, as tempting as the first choice was.

'So I'm going to be Mrs...?' I asked.

'Yıldız' he replied.

'This could be fun after all' I said and he winked.

We arrived at our room and I opened the door. Onur scooped me up, kissing my forehead and carried me across the threshold into our "honeymoon" suite. I giggled like a school girl. It was no surprise that he threw me straight onto the bed. He was right, it was definitely worth it.

We lay there for some time afterwards. It was almost two now. I'd showered and wrapped myself in the Egyptian cotton sheets and sipped the champagne which had been brought to our room with compliments from the manager. Truth be told, it wasn't champagne but the sparkling wine was delightful nonetheless. Onur lay next to me, eyes closed but awake and breathing heavily. Now this is a moment I'd like to relive.

'Happy?' I asked.

He opened one eye slightly. 'Very' he replied.

I had to admit, I was too. I could have cried a few hours ago but this, well it was the perfect ending to a day. And I was posing as Mrs. Yıldız to be. I liked the sound of that. I giggled.

'What's funny?' he asked.

'Nothing' I said, sipping the fizz and humming wedding tunes in my head.

It was silly but I suppose we have to be silly from time to time. Life is too serious.

I had the best sleep. High on the notion of a fake proposal and one too many glasses of bubbly, I woke with a smile. Onur had already jumped in the shower. I stretched. The water stopped and he poked his head round the corner.

'You are my sunshine, my only sunshine' he sang.

Was this guy real? It was like he'd come straight from the pages of a fairy tale. Cliché as it may be, I loved it.

The honeymoon period was over. No more Mrs. Yıldız and what's more it was time to board the nightmare. I had told myself all morning to be upbeat. We'd had such a lovely evening and I didn't want to spoil that. We stepped onto the bus to realise that it was in fact a different one. I checked that we were with the right party which we were. Perhaps it won't be a nightmare after all. The air-con blasted a cool breeze, the seats clean – they even reclined – and everything smelt new. The family with the toddler had sat at the back of the bus, far from us. We had chosen to sit at the front in the seats with extra leg room, close to the television and mini-bar. There is a god and he loves me.

We passed everything from ancient ruins to stunning beaches. The television was playing an episode of *Friends*. It was a personal favourite of mine but looking out of the window was more than enough. White sandy beaches with crystal waters lay beyond the cobbled streets where artists painted.

'Rose?' asked Onur.

I must have zoned out a little.

'Yes?' I turned to face him.

104

'Are you okay?' he asked.

'I'm more than okay' I replied.

'I need tell you something' he said, stuttering a little between words.

I knew it. He was married or, worse, a wanted man. He was too good to be true and so was our week together. And for the first time he looked sheepish. He wasn't his usual smug self.

'You are the first girl I've brought home' he said.

I wasn't expecting that. The worry faded and the images of all the women he'd been with vanished. I was the first girl he was taking home to meet his family. I'd never had that pleasure with Mark, even after years of dating. I'd suggested it many a time but there was always some kind of excuse – 'They're away this weekend'; 'They're taking the dog to the vets' or my personal favourite 'They're tired'. It was exhausting keeping up with all the lies. And what's more, it made me wonder why on earth he didn't want me to meet them. Was I not good enough for their precious son? Let's not answer that question. This time it was different. He was different.

'I can't wait to meet them' I said. I was intrigued to see his home, his life.

Hours passed and I was perfectly happy staring out of the window, admiring all. Onur and I talked about what we may do this next week: walks along the harbour, meeting his friends and family – his huge family by the sounds of things – and sunset dinners. But it was his cousin's wedding

105

which I was most excited for. It sounded dreamy. It would be a three day event, filled with food, street parties, henna and dancing.

'We're here' he whispered.

Oh my. It was a harbour town. Fishing boats lined the sea and old fellows sat by the water's edge catching their supper. The sun was setting, an orange hue across the shallow waves. The smell of salt wafted through the open window. We passed a green grocery, a bakery and a few boutiques along the cobbled streets. Lemon trees lined the roads and pretty pink blossom painted the houses. Children hopscotched and skipped down the lanes. Now this is somewhere I could see myself living. It is magical.

'It's beautiful' I said.

'It is home' he replied.

'What's it called?' I asked.

'Fethiye' he answered.

And with that, we'd arrived in what wasn't far from paradise.

Chapter Eleven

The neighbourhood was quiet. Only the sound of crickets was audible in the summer air. The house was old, the white washed paint cracked. Trees shaded the building. There was not much else to say.

'It needs some work' Onur said as he knocked.

It needed a lot of work, now that was true. He looked ahead and I'd say he was a little embarrassed.

'It's cute' I said softly and he squeezed my hand.

He knocked again. This time it opened. She was stunning. Dark brown, waved hair flowed to her waist. I'd say she was twenty, her skin tanned and flawless and her smile, well that was something else. She was wearing a chiffon dress in emerald green. I couldn't take my eyes off her. She wrapped her arms around Onur's neck and he lifted her slightly off the floor. I'd never seen him look so happy. I was jealous, crazy jealous.

'Rose, this is my sister' Onur said.

How did I miss that one? They even had the same eyes. They had to be the most attractive siblings I'd seen.

'Hello, I'm Ela' she said before kissing me on each cheek and holding me close. 'Welcome to our home. Please come in.' She was like a breath of fresh air.

'You're beautiful' I said.

'And you are like an English Rose' she said, smirking at Onur.

I flashed crimson. I wondered what else he'd told her. He'd only talked of his sister once and had failed to mention her beauty, flawless English and how close they apparently were. Then again, we hadn't exactly shared our life stories had we?

The decor too was old-fashioned – not vintage either. It was certainly lived in, anything but minimalistic. Traditional patterned carpets lined the floors. I thought back to our night under the stars. He'd said that they'd had nothing growing up and I couldn't picture it until now. I'd had every doll I ever wished for and still wanted more. I doubted he'd even had more than one toy.

Ela led us into the kitchen. There was an older lady cooking over the stove. It smelt incredible, whatever it was. Jars filled with every spice known to man lined the window sills and baskets of ripe tomatoes, aubergines and chillies were stacked on the floor. There was nothing fancy about it.

No Emma Bridgewater pottery lining the shelves. It was a kitchen – plain and simple. Onur said something in Turkish and she turned around. She had a tear in her eye as she hugged her son. It was warming to see. She pinched his cheeks and kissed his face. It was like she was welcoming him home from school. There may be no money here but there was love.

He gestured towards me and said something. Ela clapped her hands together like a giddy school girl. His mother stood in front of me, looking me up and down. She was of an average height and build. Her hair was covered with a blue satin headscarf and she wore loose cotton clothes. Her face was something of beauty. She didn't appear to be wearing make-up but her complexion was faultless. Her eyes were olive, her smile loving. I'd say she wasn't quite fifty but her hands looked weathered. It was clear that she'd had a hard life. I just stood there as she judged me. I wasn't good enough for Mark so I waited with bated breath. Then, she kissed me on either cheek and hugged me tightly. Perhaps I was after all.

His father was sitting on a rocking chair in the far corner of the living room. He stood as we entered. It was different to how his mother had greeted him. Onur kissed his father's hand and raised it to his forehead. It wasn't until he'd done this that they patted each other on the back. I stepped forward and he bowed his head towards me. He was tall, slender and had the same piercing blue eyes. His skin was slightly lighter than that of his wife. He seemed older, wrinkles lay across his face. I smiled and we all sat. It wasn't long before his mother had made tea and brought out an array of desserts. It was quite a spread. There was baklava, a honey drizzled cake and, of course, Turkish delight. It became clear that his parents didn't speak English. I'd have loved to have spoken to them. His mum chattered away but his dad seemed to be a man of few words. Ela translated most of what was being said to my relief. I felt a little awkward as I sat there unable to contribute and unsure of what to even say. They all seemed lovely but it was different. I excused myself to use the bathroom.

'I'll show you' said Ela, jumping up.

She led me down the corridor. I had a little nosey as we went. There only seemed to be two bedrooms from the look of things. Perhaps they'd moved house since Onur had left. I couldn't help but wonder where we would sleep tonight. The bathroom was basic. The shower didn't have a screen – more of a wet room I'd say. There was a hole in the floor in the corner. I looked around for the toilet. There wasn't one. I looked over at the hole. You've got to be kidding me? I squatted, trying to find the best angle – trust me there isn't one – and debated my life.

As I walked back down the corridor, I noticed some old photographs on the wall. There was a black and white shot of what looked like his parents' wedding day. She looked beautiful. Her dress was a satin ball gown with long sleeves and she carried roses – a girl after my own heart. His

110

father looked dapper in a tailored suit, standing proudly next to his blushing bride. There was a photo of Ela as a child. Her dark ringlets were tighter than ever and her eyes sparkled to match her smile. Only a few of the photos were framed. The rest were pinned to the wall. I looked for Onur amongst the memories. There was a little crinkled picture of a young boy building a sandcastle. He had a cheeky grin, chubby cheeks and bright eyes. It was him, my little love.

'What are you doing?' Onur said.

I jumped. 'Look at you' I said, pointing at the photo. 'You're so cute.'

'And I am not cute now?' he asked, smirking.

'Well of course you are' I replied and winked his way.

'Come' he said.

He led me into one of the bedrooms. It was pink. There was a single bed in the corner and the duvet had sunflowers on it.

'This isn't your room is it?' I asked, teasing him.

He laughed. 'It is not my colour' he said, picking up a lipstick from the dresser.

There was a wardrobe, a mirror and a couple of shelves. Ten or so books, a lamp and empty perfume bottles lined these. And that was about it. The room itself was pretty small but still. I thought back to my bedroom. I'd lost count of how much I had given to charity shops over the years. I'd had everything. Perhaps they had de-cluttered in the move I thought.

'When did your parents move?' I asked.

Onur frowned. 'They've never moved. We have lived all my life here' he said.

'Oh' I said, confused.

'What?' he asked.

'Well, where is your bedroom?'

He looked down. 'I don't have a room' he said. He wouldn't look at me.

He didn't have a room? How could that be? I wanted to ask but he obviously didn't want to talk about it and I didn't want to pry. I opened my bag, arranging my things. We would be here for a week and I hated living out of a suitcase. I piled the essentials to one side and placed the cosmetics on the dresser. Ela's things were everywhere – obviously as it was her room. Perhaps I'd have to live out of my suitcase after all. I hung a few dresses which I knew would crease in the wardrobe amongst her clothes. I couldn't help but have a sneak peak of her closet. Truth be told, there were some lovely things but then again she would look stunning regardless of what she was wearing.

'Rose' Onur said softly.

He hadn't moved. He was still looking at the floor. I walked over to him and sat on his knee. I lifted his chin and gazed into his eyes.

'I was nine when Ela was born' he began. 'We had no money. She wanted a bedroom, a pink bedroom. One day she came to home crying. The girls at school laughed. I sold some things and buy pink paint. She had her pink bedroom. Her dream had come true.'

I kissed his cheek, speechless.

'I would do anything for Ela. I want to change this fortune. I told you this. And trust me, I would do anything for you' he said.

'I know' I replied.

The love he held for his sister was something else. He thought it was his job to provide for her and now he wanted to do the same for me.

'So where did you sleep?' I couldn't help but ask.

'The sofa' he said.

I kissed him once more and held him close.

I hadn't been awake long but the scent of cooking drifted through the house. Onur slept peacefully. He hadn't stirred once. I let him be and got dressed. I stretched a little. It had been a long time since I'd slept in a single bed. I think I was only eight or so when my parents had bought me a king sized bed filled with goose down goodness. God I missed it. I pictured Onur sleeping on the sofa – a two-seater I hasten to add – night after night for at least half a decade. I admired him. I brushed out the curls in my hair to make loose waves, cleansed my face and dabbed Chanel on my neck. I changed into a white maxi dress before braving the toilet once more.

'Good morning' beamed Ela as we crossed paths in the hall. 'Are you hungry?' she asked.

Truth be told, I was ravenous. Come to think of it, I hadn't eaten properly in the past couple of days. And I didn't want to pass on that smell – whatever it may be. I nodded and Ela led me into the kitchen. Their mum was hunched over the stove once more. I sat at the wooden table in the corner. Ela leaned out of the window and picked a handful of oranges from the tree and began squeezing to make juice. Her mum placed dishes down on the table. There was everything from olives and figs to cheese and eggs. Several terracotta pots were filled with tomatoes, honey and different flavoured jams which tottered on the edge of the table. She placed freshly baked *simit* in a basket along with a selection of pastries. And then there were homemade chips, what looked like spicy sausage and *menemen*. It certainly was a spread like no other.

'Wow' I managed.

Ela smiled. 'The best part of the day' she said.

Ela and I tucked into the feast. It was incredible. The tomatoes were ripe, the bread warm and doughy and the eggs seasoned to perfection. Their mum packed a handful of walnuts and ate a little bread.

'What's your mother's name?' I asked Ela.

'Gül' she said, smirking. 'It means Rose, just like yours.'

I was stunned. It was poetic. The twist you'd expect to find in a love story.

It wasn't long before Onur joined us. He still looked sleepy.

'Morning' he said, kissing me on the forehead.

He tucked in, savouring every mouthful. I guess he'd missed home cooking, as did I. I'd been dreaming of my grandma's apple pie and custard for quite some time now.

'What are you two love birds doing today?' asked Ela.

I turned to Onur and he shrugged.

'The day is young' he said.

We sat for some time chatting once breakfast was over. I offered to help wash the dishes several times but his mum was having none of it. I can imagine she'd done everything for both Onur and Ela when they were little and didn't want to stop now. She seemed content to have him home again. Onur showered and dressed whilst I freshened up. I now had a little pot belly but it was so worth it. I was looking forward to tomorrow morning already.

It was midday by the time we left the house and the summer sun was baking down on us. Onur was wearing denim shorts, a white cotton t-shirt and flip flops. We walked hand in hand along the dusty lanes, shaded by lemon and olive trees.

'I love your family' I said, swinging his arm back and to.

He grinned and I couldn't help but think back to the photo of him as a little boy.

'They love you too' he said.

I'd love to know what they had said about me but I didn't want to ask.

'And you never told me that your mum and I have the same name' I added.

He lifted my hand to his lips and kissed it tenderly. I had a skip in my step as we walked on. The air was fresh, the grass green. Chickens clucked across our path and there were a few goats ahead. I hadn't pictured it like this. It was so very different to Istanbul. Iris, a good friend of mine, lived in Cheshire. I'd visited her a few times and it was a breath of fresh air to escape to the country. Her house was a converted barn amongst lavender fields. We would take a picnic to the nearby meadow, drink Pimm's in the spring sunshine and watch the cows graze on the grass. I loved London – that goes without saying. Every week there was a new art exhibition or Thai restaurant opening. It was never dull but oh how I loved the country.

It was only ten minutes or so before we were at the harbour. The sound of the water was soothing. I took a deep breath as we passed the locals catching their daily fish on the docks. There was a charming restaurant close by which served seafood and well, it couldn't get much fresher than that could it? I made a note and hoped to eat there before the week was through. There were a few cafés and an ice-cream parlour. Locals rode bicycles along the waterfront. A lady rode by with fresh flowers and a newspaper in her basket. There was a row of benches, shaded by blossom trees, looking out to sea.

'Shall we sit here?' I asked.

Onur nodded and we sat under the shade, his arm wrapped around my shoulder. I nested into him. Everything was perfect. We chatted about his family a little and then sat there in silence. I looked ahead, watching a fishing boat bob along the waves.

'Onur' someone called.

I looked around and she was coming over to us, calling his name yet again. Onur jumped up, kissing the woman on either cheek. Who the hell was she?

Chapter Twelve

I knew that she couldn't be another sister – he only had the one – but perhaps she was his cousin? That was wishful thinking. They'd be talking for quite some time now and he hadn't yet introduced me to the mystery woman. She had short glossy hair, red lips and was wearing a black midi dress. Her figure was incredible and she looked so very chic. I looked out to sea. He'd made it clear that he wanted me to be his but I couldn't seem to shake the idea of the "many women" that he'd been with. How many was *many* anyway?

It was another few minutes before they said their goodbyes and she walked onwards. Onur meandered back. I was green with envy but I tried to play it cool. I wasn't sure if it was the girl, their body language or the fact that I was invisible through it all. Onur put his arm around me but I pulled away. I couldn't look at him. I was overreacting, a little maybe, but I felt foolish.

'What's wrong?' he finally asked.

I took a deep breath and turned to face him. Perhaps I was being a tad dramatic. I looked at him and there were red stained lips on his cheek.

'How many other girls do you want to be yours?' And just like that, I'd blurted out exactly what I was thinking.

Onur looked ahead. His nostrils flared slightly, he looked angry. He didn't say anything. We sat there in silence and for the first time it was awkward. I twisted the ends of my hair, listening to his shallow breathing. The fishing boat had since docked, the elderly gentleman offloading his catch for the day. I don't know why but I felt guilty. I felt like I should apologise but I wouldn't be the first to speak. I guess Onur had the same thought. We sat there in a tense silence for the best part of forty minutes. It should have been the perfect evening. The sea air was fresh, we were shaded beneath the blossom trees and the sun kissed our feet. I was itching to say something but as time went on it became harder to utter a word.

'Rose' Onur whispered.

Thank god for that I thought. I turned to face him. He'd since rubbed his face, smudging the lipstick into his skin.

'Do you trust me?' he then asked.

Truth be told, I wasn't quite sure. I'd known this man just over a week. He'd ticked all the right boxes but I just didn't know. I wasn't the best judge of character after all. I'd learned that after Mark. Mark had been sleeping with Sophie on the side for the best part of two months before I'd found them at it on his kitchen floor. She was the only one I knew of but it soon became clear that there had been many. The hurt came flooding back.

'Rose, do you trust me?' he repeated when I hadn't responded.

'I'm scared' I said softly.

'Scared?' he asked, frowning.

'I don't want to be hurt again. I can't go through that again' I murmured.

I couldn't help it but tears ran down my face. Onur pulled me close and this time I let him. I sobbed.

'That girl is an old friend' he began and I listened. 'We went to school together. We kissed, one kiss, not more. I was sixteen. Her mother is die, her father is not well. She asks me for help. She can't pay the hospital bill so I send her money for this. That is all, trust me.'

Here was my very own Mr. Right acting like Robin Hood and I was being a total cow.

'So, do you trust me?' he asked again.

I didn't need to say anything. He was moons apart from Mark. I pressed my lips to his and lost myself in the moment.

We sat in the same spot until the sun became a red blanket across the sea. The sky bled into the mountains. There was a slight nip in the air now. We walked hand in hand along the harbour, down the dusty lanes and back to his home.

Ela opened the door. The smell of home cooking drifted through the house. I could get used to this.

'Did you have a nice day?' she asked, beaming. She always seemed upbeat.

'Yes, it was lovely' I replied and Onur squeezed my hand.

'Are you hungry?' he asked.

Frankly, I was still full from the banquet this morning but I wouldn't say no to his mother's cooking.

It wasn't the usual dinner party setting. We sat on the floor in the living room around a low wooden table. There was rice, stuffed vine leaves and aubergines filled with what looked like chilli. Freshly baked bread lay in a basket. It was still warm and doughy. There was no cutlery, everyone ate with their hands. The food was incredible. She made something so simple taste so delicious.

'Rose, are you excited for tomorrow?' Ela asked.

I frowned. 'What's tomorrow?'

'It's the wedding!' she exclaimed.

'I thought the wedding was on Saturday?'

'It is but it starts tomorrow. It's a three day thing.'

Oh yes, the three day celebration. I hadn't even thought about what I would wear. I'd need three outfits.

'So what happens tomorrow?' I asked.

I was so excited for the wedding. It sounded like an Indian celebration, what with the henna and dancing. I'd been to my fair share of English weddings and they were all beautiful – fairy-tale endings in country gardens. It was clear that Ela loved a good wedding. She'd explained all. Tomorrow would be the first day of the celebrations. There would be a street party mid afternoon with music and food. Day two would be the henna evening and day three is the wedding. It sounded magical. I'd asked Ela what I should wear for the different days and she said she'd help me decide.

Onur hadn't spoken much and his parents had chatted amongst themselves. I helped Ela and her mum take the dishes through to the kitchen, even though she insisted on doing it herself. I headed back into the living room. Onur and his father were talking. I'd hardly seen them speak since we'd been here. They were deep in conversation so I thought I'd leave them to it and headed into the bedroom. I sat on the bed and checked my phone. I sent a quick text to Mum and Eve – they'd be worrying – and scanned over the other messages I was yet to reply to. I'd see everyone next week anyway but I loved reading messages from home. I felt warm inside. Onur knocked on the open door.

'Hey' I said.

'You okay?' he asked.

I nodded and smiled his way.

'Listen, I'm sorry about earlier' I began but before I could say more he spoke.

'Forget this Rose. I will never hurt you. That's a promise.' And I believed him. 'Are you tired?' he then asked.

'A little' I replied.

The day had felt long. It was past ten anyway. He shut the door behind him and planted a tender kiss on my forehead. I longed for him. It had felt like an eternity since our bodies had touched. I inhaled his scent as his lips touched my neck. I pulled his t-shirt up but he stopped me.

'Not now' he said, sternly so.

I get it. It was his parents' house, his sister's bedroom and it wasn't like we were engaged or anything – well not truly anyway. But I only had another six days with him. Would we even see each other again? We hadn't spoken about it. I suppose it would be a long distance relationship. Would that even work? God knows.

'I want you' I whispered.

'Soon' he said.

It better be sooner rather than later. Needless to say, it was exciting. We were sixteen again. As I closed my eyes I thought of all the places he would ravish me. Sex on the beach was a little cliché I must admit. And with that thought, I dreamed of my very own dreamboat.

It must have been early. I could hear a rooster crowing in the distance. Onur was fast asleep. There was a dull thudding sound. It was coming from outside. I drew back the curtains. There was about five or so men with drums and instruments at the end of the street. And so the wedding began.

Ela warned me that today's event wasn't as dressy as I'd first thought. I'd asked for her opinion on a polka dot slip and courts. She said it was stunning but no. Today was more casual, about family before the big day. She picked out a simple nude dress which flowed past the knee. She wore a pair of jeans and a crimson blouse. Ela and her parents had already made their way outside to the party. The drumming was louder than ever. I perched on the edge of the bed as Onur woke. He'd slept for at least ten hours and looked as though he wanted more.

'Morning' I said, kissing his cheek.

He pulled me on top of him. 'Soon enough?' he asked, winking.

Was he kidding? I was ready for the party but how could I say no? Who knew when we would next get the chance and I desperately wanted him. He kissed me, his tongue searching for mine. He threw me down on the bed and mounted me. He was already naked. Oh how he'd planned this. I held him close, the weight of him heavy on top of me. He pulled my dress over my head, baring my breasts. Our bodies moved in unison. His chest grazed my nipples as he moved back and forth. I was close. It was a sensation like no other. I came loudly and he put his hand other my mouth. He moved a little more before falling beside me. It was incredible as ever.

We stepped outside. I had to reapply most of my make-up and re-curl my hair but it was worth it. We held hands as we walked into the crowd. There must have been at least two hundred people in the street, maybe even more. The drummers were still banging away, whilst a violinist and saxophonist played the melody. I'd always loved jazz but this was far from that. Traditional Turkish music echoed through the streets. Neighbours listened from their balconies. There was a marquee close by filled with huge terracotta pots. I had a little nosey as we walked past. There was rice, yoghurt, meat stews, roasted vegetables and every type of mezze known to man. The smell was something else. It certainly was a wedding feast. Some people danced to the beat, others chatted away. The elderly sat on plastic chairs outside their homes. We weaved in and out of the crowd. Ela could be seen a mile away. She was dancing, her hair blowing in the breeze. We joined her before Onur excused himself to chat with his friends. Ela pointed out a few of their relatives. I'd met two uncles, an aunt, four cousins and a lot of family friends in a matter of minutes. Their family was huge. It certainly was a big, fat, Turkish wedding.

Lunch was served. Now this was the part I was looking forward to. People sat on their plastic chairs and perched on fences. Ela and I made our way to the marquee. I helped myself to a little of everything. It was certainly different to sausage rolls and finger sandwiches. I'd always loved a good buffet but this was on another level. Our plates overflowing, we sat on the wall outside her house. The food was some of the best I'd ever tasted. It took me back to the kebab stall in Istanbul. It was authentic Turkish food with heart and soul mixed in. I looked across at Onur. He was with a few other guys his age, maybe friends from school. He looked my way and winked. Ela saw this too.

'You like him?' she asked.

It seemed like a silly question but I guess she was looking out for her big brother.

'Of course' I replied.

'He really likes you. He hasn't stopped talking about his English Rose' she said, beaming.

It was what I needed to hear after yesterday.

'He's not had much luck in life, or love, until now.'

What did she mean? Had he too had his heart broken?

'Do you think he's the one?' she then asked, her eyes widening.

She must have watched one too many romantic films. But for the first time, without delay, I knew the answer.

'I think he is.'

Chapter Thirteen

The saxophonist serenaded all into the early evening, lulling people with soft jazz. Ela and I had chatted for what felt like hours. She really was a breath of fresh air. Onur laughed with his friends nearby. He seemed carefree, happy. Why had he gone to Istanbul? Surely there were closer places to study. Why anyone would want to leave this place was beyond me. The streets were filled with nothing but love and joy. The happy couple were in the midst of the crowd. The bride had chestnut wavy locks which flowed down her back and wore a smile a mile long. She was on top of the world and I didn't blame her. The groom danced by her side. He was groomed – ignore the pun – and dressed in a cotton shirt and slacks. He looked at her with pride. They must have been in their late twenties and seemed madly in love. I spent the rest of the evening floating on a sea of flatbread, hummus and happiness.

If I ever get married, I too want a three day celebration. When I was little I'd drag my birthday out for at least a week – okay I still did so but who doesn't? The cake is normally cut at a wedding before you even recall the magic of the day. It flashes by in an instant. Don't get me wrong, I'd love to hear church bells, sing hymns and have a country garden bouquet but this type of wedding may just be the latest trend.

The next day, neighbours tidied the streets and decorated for celebration number two. It was dusk before we knew it. Lanterns hung over the street and the marquee twinkled with fairy lights. There were hundreds of people – some faces I recognised and others seemed new. I'd let Ela choose something for me to wear. She picked out the red velvet dress that I'd worn on my date with Onur. I was going to wear something different but it was a fabulous dress. Onur wore a white shirt, black trousers and tan loafers. He looked dapper. Ela looked stunning as always and his parents were dressed to impress. Musicians played traditional Turkish songs. There was no sign of the bride and groom. No one was dancing. It seemed that we were awaiting their arrival.

'I'm excited' I said to Onur.

I really was. He kissed my cheek. It wasn't long before the groom could be seen welcoming guests. He was wearing a navy suit with a red tie and a pocket handkerchief.

He shook the hands of many men and kissed the hands of his elders. I cranked my neck looking for the bride.

'Where is she?' I whispered.

Onur frowned.

'The bride' I said, a little sarcastically.

'She will come' he said.

I found it strange that they weren't together but then again, a lot of things were different here. I wondered what her dress would be like. The wedding gown would surely be saved for the big day. Perhaps it would be another white gown. I loved the idea of having an outfit change for an evening reception. Ivy, a family friend, wed Ted in a lace, strapless gown but then changed into a satin, ivory jumpsuit late afternoon. That was a fabulous wedding. They'd wed in a meadow filled with daffodils in late spring. The flower girls carried baskets filled with lemon roses and Ivy held a bouquet of calla lilies. It was everything a wedding should be. The cake was made from cheese – tiers of brie, Cornish Yarg, stilton and smoked cheddar. There were cupcakes iced with *I do* and they danced to '*When a Man Loves a Woman*'. Ivy and Ted had since separated but that was beside the point. I pictured the brides' hands covered with henna. Ela said that we too could have our hands painted. I'd seen Indian henna before and it was an art. It would be lovely to take a little bit of Turkey back home. The groom danced in the middle of the marquee with close friends and the drumming began.

'She's coming' Onur said.

And there she was. Oh my. It was nothing like I'd imagined. There was no satin jumpsuit. She was wearing a red gown adorned with gold jewels. Her head was covered with red lace and her train flowed behind her. The groom held his hand out for hers and they danced under the stars. Everyone watched in awe. I had a Cheshire Cat grin across my face. It was nothing but magic. It took me back to when Onur and I danced beneath the stars. It may sound soppy but it really is the thing of dreams. Mark thought that money bought romance and gone are the days of the high school dances that my grandma would tell me of. Grandad would call on her every Saturday and they'd jive their way into the late evening. She told me that they were high on love and that truly is the only way to describe it.

'Want to dance?' asked Onur. Other couples were now joining the bride and groom.

'I'd love to' I replied, taking his hand.

He spun me around and we slow danced for what felt like a lifetime. His hand was on my lower back, his other holding my palm. I rested my head on his shoulder as our feet moved. His parents swayed next to us. They looked so in love.

The music soon changed. Everyone began clicking their fingers and moving to the beat. Ela cut in and danced between us. She looked incredible. I followed her move. It was relatively simple. Onur pulled a white handkerchief from his pocket and linked fingers with another guy. Ela stood back and clapped. One by one, the men began dancing in unison. The beat picked up and they moved faster and faster. Onur had the biggest grin on his face. I clapped and he winked. He waved the handkerchief and more men joined. It looked to be the Turkish equivalent of the Conga. The groom joined too and everyone cheered. Onur came over to me once they'd finished. He was panting.

'Impressed?' he asked, smug as ever.

'Very' I replied.

'Do you want to walk?' he asked.

I had to admit it was very hot and crowded and I wouldn't pass on some alone time with my blue-eyed boy. I nodded. He loosened his tie and flung his jacket over his shoulders as they do in the movies and we weaved in and out of the crowd. There were even people dancing two streets over. How did someone know this many people? Ted and Ivy had a hundred guests at their wedding and I thought that was a lot. I chuckled.

'What?' Onur asked.

'There are so many people' I said.

'Wait for tomorrow' he replied.

Surely there couldn't be many more guests? I wondered where the big day would be – a castle perhaps. I couldn't see it taking place in a daffodil field that's for sure. We sauntered down another dusty lane, hand in hand. There were no more crowds, the music quieter. Onur stopped. He turned to face me.

'Be mine?' he asked softly.

131

I wondered if he'd asked Ela to ask those questions yesterday. I'd like to think he was the one but how would it work? I was flying home in a matter of days and who knew when our paths would cross again, if ever. I twisted my hair between my fingertips.

'Rose' he persisted.

'Onur, I like you, I really do' I said. 'I just can't answer that question now.'

It was the truth. It would be wrong to string him along, especially if he'd had his heart broken before. Everything was perfect as it was. It felt like the fairy tale. He kicked the dirt and breathed heavily.

'I am yours' I said and kissed him tenderly on the lips. 'I will give you an answer before I leave.'

'Deal' he replied.

'Come on, let's make the most of tonight' I said and we strolled back down the lanes.

People were still dancing. I spotted Ela in the distance and we made our way over to her. The bride and groom were now sat in the middle of the marquee. An elderly woman stood in front of them with a terracotta pot.

'It's time for the henna' whispered Ela.

It couldn't have been any further from what I'd imagined. This was far from art. There were no intricate patterns. It was a just a blob of ink. The elderly woman pressed what I assumed to be the henna onto the bride's palms and covered them with satin gloves.

'Is that it?' I asked, underwhelmed.

Ela nodded. 'It's our turn' she said.

I'd gone on about how excited I was for the henna and now I was going to be stuck with an orange spot on my palm for the best part of three weeks – fabulous.

'This is our grandmother' Ela said, gesturing to the elderly lady.

She must have been eighty or so but she was cute. She wore cotton trousers and a silk headscarf. Her skin was weathered but her eyes sparkled nonetheless. She grabbed my hand, placed the henna in the centre and pressed down slightly. She then kissed my cheek. It seemed like she was the heart of the family. She was the glue which held everything together and it reminded me of my grandma. Love is really all you need.

Ela placed a red, silk scarf over her head and did the same to me. She pushed me into the middle and we started dancing around the happy couple. I looked back at Onur and he smiled. I didn't have a clue what was happening. Other women joined with tambourines and a few were even belly dancing. All that we needed now was a snake charmer. It felt like something out of *Aladdin*. Perhaps Onur and I would travel high and low on a magic carpet after all.

The bride stood and danced around her husband-to-be. This went on for some time and the crowd clapped and cheered. I felt silly but no one here seemed fazed. Onur's grandmother gave his cousin a terracotta vase. It looked heavy. She danced with it for some time before smashing it on the floor into a thousand pieces. The jewels covered the dusty street. Every child ran in to collect their treasure. The boiled sweets glistened like rubies in the twinkling lights. The groom stood and took his bride from the circle. He threw the lace veil back and kissed her forehead. She looked beautiful. Her hair was in a chignon, a few curls loose at the sides. She had smoky eyes, blushed cheeks and a deep red across her lips. She pressed her hands to his, leaving an orange residue on his palms. It now seemed that they were one. The streets were filled with applause and then the party really started.

I was exhausted. Turks really know how to throw a party. The dancing continued into the wee hours of the morning. It struck me odd that there was not a drop of alcohol in sight. Everyone was in fact high on love and food for that matter. Barbecued meats, homemade bread and yoghurt and herb dip. It was simple but incredible. Then there was the drink. I can't say I was a fan but I guess it was an acquired taste. It looked like milk but was frothy and tasted like a mix of yoghurt and salt water. I pulled the most unattractive face and Onur took it from me, much to his mother's dislike. I swear that everyone I met was another relative, normally a cousin. I certainly didn't feel invisible tonight. And then, there she was.

It was the girl from the other day – his childhood sweetheart. She kissed Onur on the cheek, smudging a pink into his stubble. Ela hugged her and they chatted for some time. I know they'd only kissed once, maybe more, but it riled me that she knew his family. I thought I was the first girl he'd brought home? I started to feel like that invisible girl once more. She was wearing a rather revealing dress and the highest of heels. She had a killer pair of legs. Onur spoke to her and then I heard my name. He gestured towards me and she looked straight across. She seemed to hesitate but soon came over and kissed me on either cheek. There was warmth in the kiss, no jealousy. It was nice to be seen. Onur glanced at me and pulled me back into the dancing crowd. There was no awkward silence this time that was for sure. I guess I didn't have anything to worry about after all.

It wasn't long after that we called it a night. The sound of drumming and tambourines could still be heard as a few danced the night away.

'My feet are so sore' I moaned as we got into bed.

These courts had always bruised my feet but they were pretty.

'I kiss better' Onur said.

He began rubbing my feet and I giggled as he tickled the sole of my foot. But he didn't stop there. He licked the inside of my leg up to my inner thigh.

'I thought we couldn't?' I said, confused.

He placed his finger over my lips. And then he kissed every inch of my body.

Chapter Fourteen

I'd woken from the dreamiest of dreams. Who knew that orgasms – yes multiple – were the answer to insomnia. In London, I'd toss and turn for most of the night, awake with my thoughts but not here. I had lost myself in a sea of serenity. The sex was incredible, as always. I'd bit my lip to stay quiet. Onur had put his hand over my mouth – a turn on in itself. There was no lock on the door. It took me back to when Samuel and I would do "homework" in his room. His mum would come upstairs with blueberry muffins fresh from the oven and I'd quickly hide my bra under his bed. I'd always felt naughty but this was something else. I felt alive. Onur was sound asleep, breathing deeply. I kissed him softly on the cheek and he stirred ever so slightly. I tiptoed down the hallway to the bathroom. The water was an aphrodisiac, caressing my body with its warmth. I lathered the olive soap and blew a bubble. It drifted out of the open window. When I was little, Mum told me to make wishes with the bath bubbles and it was something I still did. She'd always believed in a little magic.

I twisted my hair into a towel, wrapped another around myself and snuck back into the bedroom. I let it drop, baring all and massaged lotion over my body. I'd caught the sun. I'd always turned a faint shade of pink but a glow now washed over my skin and I couldn't help but admire the sun-kissed me. There were a few freckles across my cheeks and my hair had lightened. I am fabulous. And for the first time in as long as I can remember, I believed it.

'Well, good morning' Onur said in a deep voice. 'Nice view.' He winked, staring at my behind.

I gave him a little twirl and he pulled me onto the bed. He kissed me tenderly, gawking at the nudity.

'Did you sleep well?' I asked softly.

'Too well' he answered.

Sex may make things complicated but it was worth it. I'd considered celibacy after Mark – a tad dramatic I know – but why would anyone pass on this? The towel had since dropped, my wet hair now dripping over my breasts and running down to my navel. Onur licked the water and went a little further down. He slapped my bare bottom.

'Again?' he asked.

The answer was most certainly yes.

The morning passed. He'd served me up yet another orgasm before breakfast. We'd gorged our way through brunch –

banquet more like. I'd indulged in figs, goat's cheese and honey on freshly baked bread. All in all, it was a morning filled with pleasures. Today was the big day. It was the last day of the celebrations and, dare I say it, half way through the week. The wedding didn't begin until eight this evening which I thought a little odd. Ela said we could get a sneak peak of the happy couple before they were whisked away for photographs – just the two of them. I loved this idea. I pictured intimate shots of the newlyweds strolling down the beach, the sun and waves as their backdrop. Ivy had cursed her mother-in-law after their wedding as she'd wanted to be in almost every shot and kept fixing Ted's tie. I always wondered whether she was one of the reasons for the separation but never dared to ask. There would be none of that here. It would just be the two of them, how it is meant to be.

The drumming began. The dull echo was soon joined by a saxophone and a string quartet. People gathered in the street and on their balconies for a glimpse of the bride. I'd always been obsessed with wedding gowns. *Vogue* had captured the beauty over the years and I fell in love with the weddings of Grace Kelly and Lady Diana. The dress aside, it's a bride's smile that does it for me. It is the day of your dreams. And there she was. The dress was ivory satin in an a-line silhouette. The train, adorned with buttons, was at least two foot long. She wore a lace veil which flowed to the floor and held red roses tied with white ribbon. Her hair was in loose curls, her lipstick the same shade as her bouquet.

She wore pearl earrings. She was stunning, she was classic. The groom held her hand, his smile as wide as hers. He wore a dinner suit, dicky bow and all. He led his bride into the street as they swayed to the jazz. No one else danced. This day was theirs. The neighbours watched on as the happy couple danced beneath the sun. Onur took my hand in his and kissed it, the look of love in his eyes.

The bride and groom soon drove off into the sunset – quite literally – in a convertible dressed with ribbons. Onur and I spent the rest of the day at his home. We sat in the garden amid the orange trees and I drifted in and out of sleep.

'She looked beautiful' I said, my head in his lap.

'Not as beautiful as you' he replied, kissing my forehead.

I smiled and looked around the garden. Mint and tomatoes were growing and orange and lemon trees shaded all. Pink blossom covered the kitchen door and terracotta plant pots lined the doorstep. It was serene. The sky was now a deep red, the air cooler. The clouds blew across the skyline. I'd lost track of how long we'd been sitting here.

'We should get ready' I sighed, reluctant to move.

Onur nodded and we made our way inside.

Onur wore a dinner suit with shiny dress shoes. He looked dapper. I wore a satin slip dress in ivory with navy polka dots and black courts. I dabbed my neck with Chanel and stained my lips a deep red.

'Ready?' he asked. I nodded.

'You look wonderful' he said softly and I blushed.

'So do you' I replied.

He winked and took my hand. I had to admit, we made a pretty good-looking couple.

Ela looked incredible. She was wearing an off the shoulder black gown which nipped in at her waist. Her hair was twisted into a messy bun, her make-up classic. Their dad wore a suit, nothing special but he looked smart enough and their mother looked radiant in a long-sleeved black dress and green headscarf. Onur opened the car door for me and joined me on the backseat. He placed his hand on my knee and his arm around my shoulder. I leaned into him as we made our way down the lanes. Ela was like a giddy school girl. She had chatted all the way there – well it wasn't far at all. There was traffic ahead, bright lights and beeping.

'What's happening?' I asked.

'The wedding' Onur replied.

The cars lined the streets, sounding their horns and flashing their lights in celebration – the norm as it seemed. It was an open area with cobbled floors, adorned with fairy lights and a blanket of stars in the night sky. It was simple but beautiful. The tables were covered with white linen and pillar candles and ivory bows were tied on each chair. The top table was covered in rose petals and tea lights. Everything twinkled. It was a fairy-tale wedding. Hundreds of people were already there. Onur introduced me to more of his distant relatives. And there it was in the middle of the room. The cake was seven tiers, iced with rose petals. It was unlike anything I'd seen. It was most certainly a showstopper.

'Would you like a drink?' Onur asked.

'Absolutely' I replied.

I wasn't one of those girls that drank a lot. I'd be happy with one or two gin and tonics. Mark had always called me his cheap date. Oh how I loathed him. We made our way to the bar. It was a wooden hut and an oval pool lay behind it. Onur ordered himself a drink, whiskey was his poison as it seemed.

'What would you like?' he asked.

'Champagne please' I said.

The bartender nodded and poured a glass of fizz into a flute.

'Cheers' I said as we chinked our glasses together. I took a sip and the bubbles popped on my tongue.

Ela made her way over to us. She said something to Onur and he shook his head. She pleaded like a little girl. She soon turned on her heel in a huff and made her way back into the crowd.

'What was that all about?' I asked.

'She wants alcohol' he said.

I couldn't see the problem. She in her twenties and we were at a wedding. There must be more to it than that.

'It is not our religion to drink' he said.

'Is that water?' I asked sarcastically, motioning to his glass.

'I don't play by rules' he replied, smugly.

'Of course you don't' I said, taking another sip.

He was everything rolled into one. He was the bad boy, smug and full of himself. He was the romancer, the dancer, the seducer. He was respectful, loving and someone I could see myself growing old with. I couldn't help but wonder which one truly defined him. Then again, I didn't care. This handsome man was standing next to me and saying all the right things.

'Another?' he asked – see, all the right things.

'Please' I replied, handing him the empty glass.

I took a sip, tipsy on love and twinkling lights. The band was playing classical music. More and more guests arrived, filling the tables. Onur and I sat on a table with his family. The music soon stopped and everyone was quiet. You could have heard a pin drop. The drumming began and the bride and groom entered, walking down a red carpet amongst the hundreds of guests. I still couldn't believe how many people were here. Everyone applauded and whistled. Fireworks filled the sky, lighting up the night. The groom led his wife-to-be onto the dance floor where they swayed under the moonlight. It really was what dreams are made of. She looked radiant. Others began to join the happy couple and slow danced. Onur stood and held his hand out for mine.

'Dance with me' he said.

I'd never grow tired of dancing with this man. I rested my head on his shoulder as we swayed in the light of the moon. His touch was warming. I was happy. The beat picked up a little and people danced the night away. We'd been dancing for the best part of an hour by this point.

'Tired?' Onur asked.

'A little' I said, nodding.

We sat at the table once more. Onur had gone to the bar for more drinks. I couldn't remember if this was my sixth or seventh glass of fizz now but I felt fabulous. Ela was still dancing in the midst of the courtyard. Onur's mother looked at me. I'd love to know what she was thinking. I still wasn't sure if she liked me or not. It was difficult. We were worlds apart. Onur and his sister would translate a few things I'd said but it just wasn't the same. I smiled her way and she bowed her head towards me. Onur came back with the drinks and I floated on bubbles once more. He spoke with his parents, holding my hand. I looked ahead. The guests looked wonderful. The men were all suited and booted and the women were dressed in vivid silks. There was a little boy, wearing a linen suit and bobbing to the music.

The bride and groom sat at the top table and everyone else took their seats. There was no aisle and no music. They sat hand in hand. I couldn't understand a word but I got the gist. *'Will you take this man to be your lawfully wedded husband?'* She nodded with a tear in her eye. *'Will you take this woman to be your lawfully wedded wife?'* He said *'I do'*, they kissed and lived happily ever after. The place filled with applause and tears.

The guests began lining up to congratulate the newlyweds. Onur and I took our place. Each guest would kiss the bride and shake the groom's hand. They'd then pin money to his suit and her dress – very odd. It was our turn. They must have been covered in thousands by now. Ivy said she'd been given unsightly cake stands and unwanted kitchen utensils as gifts. She'd tried to take a few things back but some were non-returnable. Ted had said they shouldn't throw them away – it would be bad luck. He was right after all. This got rid of that problem. Onur gave me a note and I softly pinned it to the satin of her dress and kissed her on either cheek. He did the same to the groom. It took close to an hour for everyone to do this. The newlyweds then cut the cake. It was chocolate sponge with fresh cream and berries. I'd spied another piece but almost five tiers had since gone.

The photographer was making her way around the crowds, capturing the happy moments. I was dying to see the shots she'd taken. I'd say she was in her twenties, her blonde hair tied back in a yellow scrunchie. She was soon at our table. Onur pulled me close as we posed for our first photo together.

'Cute' she said.

'You're English?' I asked, taken aback.

'Yes. I'm Poppy' she said, pulling up a chair.

'Rose. Nice to meet you' I replied. 'Do you live here?'

'Only during the season – six months here and then six months back home. I just love life out here. Is this your boyfriend?' she asked, gesturing towards Onur.

'Kind of' I answered, hesitantly.

She was a breath of fresh air. We spoke for twenty minutes or so. She was twenty six, single and loved the eighties and peanut butter. She'd been coming here since she was a dot and fell in love with the place. Now she spent the summer months as a wedding photographer. I'd asked to see the shots from earlier today. They were beautiful and just as I'd imagined. The couple strolled hand in hand along the beach, the waves crashing behind them. The way the groom looked at his bride was magical.

'These are wonderful' I said, flicking through.

'Thank you' she replied, blushing a little.

I flicked forward to the photo of Onur and I and I couldn't help but smile. He looked insanely gorgeous and I looked, well, happy.

'I best get back but it was lovely to meet you' she said.

'And you' I replied.

Onur had since put another glass of bubbly in front of me.

'She was lovely' I said to him, slurring my words ever so slightly.

'Are you drunk Miss Jones?' he asked, smirking.

'Not at all' I replied.

Now that was a lie. I'd felt tipsy three glasses ago but I wasn't going to let on. Perhaps this should be my last glass. I took a small sip and it went straight to my head.

'Another dance?' he asked.

I'd have loved to but I wasn't sure if I could stand. The fairy lights swirled around my irises.

'Later' I replied, taking a deep breath.

He nodded and kissed my forehead.

There was a scream and clapping filled the room. I jerked my neck trying to see what was happening. The crowd soon parted. There was a man on one knee holding a ring. She jumped on him, screaming her answer. He kissed his wife-to-be and she cried tears of joy. It was like a dream. I had the cheesiest grin across my face. Oh how I loved a happy ending. Onur put his hand on my leg and kissed me.

'Do you want that?' he asked.

I was taken aback but smiled nonetheless. Of course I wanted to get married, one day.

'Marry me Rose?'

And I don't know if it was the champagne or the love but I screamed *YES*.

Chapter Fifteen

Don't panic. Don't panic. It was a dream. I remember the sixth glass of champagne. How much did I drink? Let's rewind a little. There was the ceremony, the cake and then, oh god. I'M ENGAGED! I lifted my head. It felt heavy, full of fizz. I'd agreed to marry my man of the moment, a man I'd known for the best part of a week and a half. What was I thinking? I looked to my right. He wasn't there but the sheets were slept in. Come to think of it, I couldn't remember leaving the wedding. Had he put me to bed? I fell into the pillows, my head in my hands. Oh Rose. This is not how I imagined it. I'd always pictured myself floating on cloud nine after a proposal from the man of my dreams. Instead, I was hung-over and questioning my answer. The door opened. It was him. He was dressed, carrying two cups of coffee. He leaned forward and kissed my forehead, handing me my caffeine fix.

'*Günaydın aşkım*' he said.

I smiled. He was ideal but still. Perhaps it was a joke? We would laugh it off and go back to our whirlwind, no-strings-attached romance.

'Wife' he whispered in my ear, kissing my neck – perhaps not.

I took a gulp of coffee.

'Last night was...' I began.

'A dream' he finished.

Oh I wish it was. Truth be told, it felt like a dream. He was dreamy. Cinderella didn't really know Prince Charming before he searched the kingdom for her, did she? "*A dream is a wish your heart makes*" and I'd always wished for my happy ever after so perhaps this was it. Time would tell.

I'd triple checked that I hadn't announced last night's news. I think I was too high on champagne to bother – thank goodness. I splashed my face with cold water and slipped on a jumpsuit. I brushed a pink across my lips and scrunched my curls with coconut oil. Prada was my friend today. The sunglasses covered a multitude of sins.

'Ready?' Onur asked.

I nodded. He said he'd got something planned for today. I'd planned to spend the day in bed. It was midday, the sun in its prime. He handed me a white helmet. I looked at him blankly and he gestured towards the moped. It was a

148

cherry red Vespa with a tan leather seat. I'd dreamed of riding one of these round Rome, stopping for pizza and gelato near the Spanish Steps. Today, I couldn't think of anything worse and the helmet hair was the least of my worries.

'It'll be fun' he said, winking.

His helmet wasn't as goofy as mine. Onur mounted the bike like a pro and held his hand out for mine. I climbed onto our horse and carriage and he rode off into the sun. I held him tightly as he weaved in and out of the traffic and down yet another dusty lane. He jumped a red light – bad boy.

'Are you okay?' he shouted.

'Yes!' I screamed over the engine.

In truth, it was exhilarating. The wind blew my hair and the sun warmed our skin. I held Onur. We rode past the harbour, past the fishermen and up a dirt track. There was no traffic here. He took another sharp turn upwards. Pine trees shaded us from the sun and the air was fresher. There was an opening ahead and Onur stopped. Wow, just wow. The view from the mountain was something else. The waves crashed against the rocks below. The only sound was that of crickets. We were alone and it was serene.

'It's beautiful' I said.

I stood on the mountain edge and breathed in the sea air.

'Close your eyes' he said.

'What?' I asked.

'Close your eyes' he repeated.

I did as I was told, listening to the sound of the waves.

'You can open' he said after a few minutes.

I turned around. There was a checked blanket lining the floor, strawberries and champagne. I couldn't help but smile. He must have stashed it all in his backpack.

'What's this?' I asked.

'Let's say it's a celebration' he replied, his eyes glistening in the sun.

He was something else. How could I tell him that I wasn't ready? Was I ready? I was twenty four and had always longed to settle down. It wasn't like I had many other appealing options. I could go back to the mundane single life or stay in paradise with this dreamboat and live my life. He was besotted with me and had promised me the world. He didn't have millions but he had a heart of gold – that I knew of – and that's richer than any man I'd met. Onur popped the bubbly and filled the plastic cups. I couldn't help but question if he could afford this. I felt a little guilty. More champagne, was this a good idea? Perhaps a little hair of the dog would work wonders.

'Şerefe' he said, lifting his drink to mine.

'Cheers' I repeated.

'To us' he added.

I took a sip. The bubbles hit me and quenched my thirst. Just have the one glass today Rose, I told myself. I gazed out to sea. Life here is magical. I turned back to find Onur on one knee and holding a ring.

'Rose, marry me?' he asked softly, love in his eyes.

I was speechless. He'd asked me last night but it was now real. This was my get-out-of-jail-free card. Now was the time to tell him. Just say no Rose. It was too fast. I hardly knew him but then again, how well do we really know anyone? He was perfect, to me. Should I listen to my head or my heart? Say no Rose. It's that simple. I wasn't high on champagne this time and just like that I listened to my heart and nodded. He kissed me, lifting me to meet his lips and spun me around. He slid the ring on my finger and shouted from the mountain tops. It was in true DiCaprio style – "*I'm king of the world*". And quite frankly, I felt on top of the world myself. I'm engaged and this is how I'd always imagined it.

We sat on the blanket, sipped the fizz and ate the strawberries beneath the sun. I looked down at my hand. The ring was stunning. It was a yellow gold band with a sapphire in the midst of three diamonds. It was vintage and so very me. How did he know? It reminded me of Lady Di's engagement ring – albeit a lot smaller.

'It's my grandmother's' he said as I admired it.

'It's stunning' I said. The diamonds sparkled in the sunlight – a family heirloom.

'Do you think it's too fast?' I couldn't help but ask.

'Love is love' he said, shrugging.

He was right. We can't help who we fall in love with can we? He pulled me close and kissed my neck. His lips were on mine. He touched my body, my breasts.

'What are you doing?' I asked, covering my bare nipples.

He didn't answer but smirked, kissing my skin.

'We can't. Not here!' I yelled.

'Why not?' asked Onur.

I guess he was right again. There was not a soul in sight and we'd be dots from the planes passing overhead. Why not indeed? And it wasn't quite as cliché as sex on the beach.

He lowered me down, his body on top of mine. He untied my jumpsuit and dropped his shorts. He kissed every inch of me. We moved in unison beneath the sun. I moaned, time and time again. His body met mine. And then, he stilled and chuckled.

'What?' I asked.

'We have an audience' he said.

I looked to my right. It was a mountain goat. He was staring directly at us. The bell on his neck chimed with each step he took. Then, there were two more. I let out at loudest laugh as The Three Billy Goats watched our little show.

'Carry on?' Onur asked.

'Absolutely' I replied, giggling.

The sun was lower now. We packed up our things and I blew a kiss to our goat friends. There were hundreds of dandelions lining the cliff edge. I picked two and passed one to Onur.

'What's this?' he asked, frowning.

'Make a wish' I said, blowing the fairies into the sky.

He did the same and we watched as they drifted through the breeze.

'What did you wish?' he asked.

'If I tell you, it won't come true' and I kissed him.

There was so much love in that kiss. And just like that, I was high on love once more.

It was getting late, the sun even lower as we rode down the mountain. He made a left turn and we passed a few bars. Couples walked hand in hand along the beach front. He parked the bike and we strolled along the sand. It was a stunning beach. White sand stretched as far as the eye could see and soft jazz blew through the sea air. Some were still lying on the beach, others dining in the seafood restaurants opposite. We sat down in a secluded spot on the shore. The tide was low, the waves lapping back and forth. I dipped my toes in the water. It was still warm. The sun rested on the sea, orange bleeding into red across the water. It shimmered across the waves, fading until only a pink hue lit the sky. You couldn't have timed it more perfectly, yet he had. We sat there for some time, my head resting on his shoulder, his arm around me.

'Would you like a drink?' he asked.

It wasn't a good idea. I'd told myself to only have the one glass of champagne but I'd had three. Why not? You only live once. And I'd love a Cosmopolitan – true Carrie Bradshaw style.

'Please' I said, giving him my order.

Onur made his way to the wooden beach bar ahead. It felt surreal. Things like this don't happen to ordinary people. I wondered how I'd even go about telling my parents, telling Eve. They wouldn't understand. Of course they'd be worried but they didn't know him. I'd never met anyone like him. I'd tell them but tomorrow can wait. Today, I was in my own little bubble of magic and no one could pop it.

Onur soon returned with a martini glass filled with pink goodness. It probably wasn't a good idea to mix my drinks but who cared. I was happy. He had a bottle of beer and we chinked our drinks together once more.

'To us' I said and he smiled.

'Rose, I love you' he said softly.

Of course he loved me, he'd proposed but hearing those words was magic in itself. Mark had tossed love around as if it was a Frisbee. He'd never meant it, not really. Onur had said it with such passion. It felt too soon but I'd loved every moment spent with him.

'Ditto' I replied.

He frowned, obviously he hadn't seen *Ghost*. 'And I you' I said, kissing him.

I took a sip. Oh it was delicious. The sky grew dark, a blanket of stars covering the sea. There was hardly anyone on the beach now and the music became a little louder. Fishing boats were docked on the shore ready for tomorrow's catch. The tide was calmer, the water inviting.

'Fancy a swim?' I asked, winking.

'Now?' asked Onur.

I nodded and got up, lowering my jumpsuit to show my black lace underwear. He looked at me in a daze. I paddled my feet in the water. It was cooler now.

'Are you coming?' I asked.

He stood and unbuttoned his linen shirt, showing his tanned torso. He was hot, that went without saying, and he was mine. He lowered his shorts and walked over to me. We held hands and paddled in the shallow. Then he dived into the dark waters. He even had the perfect drive. Was there anything this man couldn't do? He came to the surface and slicked his wet hair back.

'Come' he said.

I swam over to him. He held me tightly as we bobbed with the tide. His wet lips were on mine, searching my mouth. I unhooked my bra and threw it to the shore. I don't know what had come over me. Onur kissed my breasts, the salt water stinging my nipples. It was a sensation like no other. Now this was the perfect end to the perfect day.

Chapter Sixteen

Onur and I were inseparable. We spent the next few days high on love, hand in hand. We'd strolled along the beach – albeit no more late night swims – and explored the old markets. They were fabulous, well nothing like the souks of Istanbul but charming nonetheless. There was a weekly market where locals would sell fruit, vegetables, cheeses and baked goods. It reminded me a little of Covent Garden. I love to sample the local cheeses and browse the book stalls for a first edition – not that I'd ever found one. I was a sucker for second hand books. The faded text and creased pages felt like a story in itself. I dreamed of having an old wooden bookcase filled with hundreds of love stories – one day perhaps.

Onur bought some ground coffee, walnuts and a dozen eggs. There was just something about buying local produce. Everything here was local. The vegetables were fresher and there was little to no packaging. Women carried their weekly shop in hessian bags, a loaf of bread under their arm. There were a few stalls selling jewellery and art. Painters lined the harbour, sketching the waterfront. This is daily life for these people. They'd sip a coffee by the sea, browse the markets and stroll along the cobbles beneath the sun.

The days flew by. We'd rode pushbikes through the town only stopping for ice-cream – pistachio and classic vanilla. Onur's mother had spoiled us with her culinary delights and we'd taken his dog for a walk through the fields in the evening. I couldn't work out what breed she was and Onur was clueless. She had a brown and white coat, the happiest of pups. Her name was *Lokum* – Turkish delight.

I looked down at my hand. The ring was a perfect fit and sparkled under the sun. His grandmother had given it to him on her deathbed for the love of his life. And he'd chosen me. I still hadn't told a soul about our news. How could I? I'd spoken to Mum but couldn't bring myself to tell her. She'd worry and I knew it would burst the bubble. I wasn't ready to come down to earth just yet. I'd deal with it when I got home. Onur hadn't told his parents either. I thought he'd shout it from the rooftops but an engagement here wasn't quite that simple. Once the happy couple had agreed to take each other's hands in marriage, the wedding plans should be well under way. And I was not ready to be a Turkish housewife any time soon. It was our secret for now.

It was soon our last day together. I'd fly home the next morning and this would all become a dream.

'Stay with me?' Onur asked as we walked along the harbour.

I wanted to, I really did. I'd fallen in love with life again and perhaps it didn't have to be a dream. This could be my life. There was nothing waiting for me back home. I'd be single, jobless and broke.

'I can't' I replied.

'You can' he said.

There were too many questions. Where would we live? I guess we'd live in the city and come here during the holidays. It could work. Could it? I'd need a job. And then it hit me, I'd write. I'd tell the tales of the unwritten love stories amid the world and across the oceans. It would be fabulous. Still, I shook my head. It just wasn't logical.

We walked for some time and the day passed. Onur said he'd got a romantic evening planned. We went back to his home and I got ready for the last night with my beloved. I wore a halter neck black dress and Manolos. I only had the one pair but dreamed of owning more. I'd picked the royal blue Hangisi satin pumps – just like Carrie wed Big in. I felt like Cinderella in her glass slippers going to the ball. They were magical. God forbid I lost one at eight hundred pounds a pair though. Onur looked sleek in a dinner shirt and linen trousers.

'I'm a lucky man' he said, staring at me. I blushed.

'Ditto' I replied.

'This means me too, yes?' he asked. I smiled and nodded.

He took me to a quaint seafood restaurant along the harbour. It was the one I'd been fond of since day one. That's what I loved about him, he remembered every detail. We dined alfresco beside the water. It was dark, the moon lighting the night sky. Candles twinkled and fresh flowers adorned the tables. Onur placed our order.

'Happy?' he asked.

'Very' I replied, sipping the French wine and star gazing.

The evening began with garlic prawns. Salmon steak, lobster bisque and crab followed. It was heavenly, just how I'd imagined it. He definitely couldn't afford this but he never said a word. He knew that I'd wanted to come here and he'd made it happen. Onur and I held hands across the table.

'Rose, please stay?' he asked, desperation in his eyes.

I sighed. I'd love to but how could I? Then again, how could I not? We were engaged. We'd be a couple who only saw each other every few months if I went back to London. It wouldn't work. Should I stay?

'I don't know' I replied. It was the truth. I didn't know what to do.

Onur rolled his eyes.

'Let's just enjoy tonight' I said. 'Tomorrow can wait.'

He nodded and we went back to our magical evening. I'm sure we'd work something out.

It was wonderful. I was full on seafood, wine and love. We'd walked a little afterwards. Onur bowed his head at the other couples passing by. There were a few tourists, not many. I spied our bench ahead. It felt like a lifetime ago since we sat here, shaded by the blossom.

'Shall we sit?' I asked.

Onur nodded and we took a seat. It was dark ahead. Stars sparkled in the distance. I took a deep breath, inhaling the sea air.

'If I stayed, what would it be like?' I asked.

Onur's eyes lit up and we spoke for some time about our fantasy life together. We'd live in Istanbul in his apartment. He had another year of studying and then the world was our oyster. I'd said that I didn't want to travel. I wanted to live here, in his hometown. I told him how I wanted a garden with orange trees and a home filled with oak furniture. I wanted a place we could call home. I told him that I could write but he said I didn't have to work. He would work for us both and I could stay at home with the children. He wanted two children, one of each, and a dog. It was a wonderful life. It was the life I'd dreamed of. So why couldn't I say yes?

'Why?' he asked.

'I just can't, not yet' I replied.

'You love me, yes?' he asked.

'Of course' I answered. It was the truth, I did.

'Then why?' he looked hopeless.

Why indeed? I couldn't answer the question. I kissed him tenderly and squeezed his hand.

'Onur, please' I began. 'Don't ask me why, I don't know. I just can't right now.'

He looked forlorn. I lifted his chin and looked into his blue eyes.

'I will come back. I will come back to you' I said.

'Promise?' he asked softly.

'I promise' I replied.

The evening was bittersweet. It had been wonderful, as always, but we both knew this was the end. I had a heavy heart. I did love him. I wanted the happily ever after but it isn't that simple. *C'est la vie*.

I began to pack my things once we got home. The flight was at noon tomorrow. It had been three months of magic. I'd come so far. I'd found myself. And who knew that I'd fall in love? It was a love story like no other, one I'd always hold close to my heart. Onur sat on the edge of the bed as I folded my life back into the suitcase.

'Rose' he said.

I looked up. No words were needed. There was love in his eyes. I sat on his knee, brushed back his hair and kissed his lips. We were from different worlds but for a brief moment, he'd become my world. I thought back to the day we'd met. It felt like a lifetime ago. I'd become obsessed with him, his touch. He'd brought me back to life. Perhaps we'd stay in touch and have that hot affair every other year.

161

He held me tightly and looked lost. This was the perfect, no-strings-attached relationship that every guy craved. Not Onur. He wanted more. He wanted me. We didn't say much as I put the last of the clothes into the case and closed it. It was final. It was the end.

'Fancy a snack?' I said, lighting the mood.

He frowned. It was eleven thirty and we were full on seafood. I pulled the remains of the rose Turkish delight from my overnight bag.

'My favourite' he said, smirking.

'And you're my Turkish delight' I replied.

He laughed and there was a little magic once more. We fell onto the bed, holding each other. Our love may not last a lifetime but it was wonderful while it lasted.

Chapter Seventeen

We stayed awake all night. There was no point in sleeping, we both knew we would only toss and turn and neither of us wanted to think of tomorrow. I'd savour the last bit of time with my man of the moment. Onur and I lay side by side. I lost myself in his dreamy eyes. He asked me about home. We'd lived in the same house since I was a dot. It was a London townhouse with a black and white tiled porch. Wisteria covered the house in the late spring, holly bushes were covered with snow in the winter. Rose trees lined the gardens. It dated back to the eighteenth century and was full of character. It was home and always would be. Onur listened. He'd had nothing, I'd had everything. He was a village boy, I was a city girl. It would have never worked. Mark and I, well we were a match made in heaven on paper. The reality of it was a little different. Onur spoke briefly of his childhood. He'd covered his life in a matter of minutes. He had made his own luck in this life. He was humble, a family man. I adored that about him.

'What will you do?' he asked.

Truth is, I hadn't even thought about it. I'd love to write. I had so many ideas. Perhaps I'd write a blog or a novel – our fleeting love story to fill the pages. I was sure of one thing. I wouldn't go back to waiting tables. I'd worked in the same Italian restaurant for almost six years. The owners were lovely and I could eat as much Carpaccio and ravioli as I wished. I just felt like I was wasted there. I'd told Donatella – my boss not Versace – I was going on to bigger and better things. I was going to find myself, find my calling in life. She'd laughed and said I'd be back before the year was out. I didn't want to give her the satisfaction.

'I don't know' I replied honestly.

'Write' he said.

Mark always said there was no money in writing and that I should work for him. He'd joked that I'd have to sleep with the boss. I bet he said that to all the girls. Mark had a tendency to hire the same type of woman – attractive blonde. He was as deep as a puddle.

'I think I will' I said.

It was what I'd always dreamed of doing and I'd need something to keep me busy.

'And what will you do?' I asked.

'God only knows' he answered.

'The world is your oyster' I said.

'Not without you' he muttered.

I felt a little guilty. I said nothing and held him tightly. I had promised that I'd come back to him and I wanted to but in truth it was an empty promise. We both knew this was the end. Engagement ring or not, we lived very different lives.

It was almost five now.

'Are you tired?' I asked.

'No' he replied.

I was a little sleepy but I could sleep on the plane.

'Come on' I said, jumping out of bed.

Onur frowned. He stared at me in wonder as I slipped on a dress, brushed out my curls and put on a little lipstick. It was the fastest I'd ever dressed.

'What are you doing?' he asked.

'Living' I replied.

He too got dressed. We snuck out of the house like naughty teenagers and strolled down the road. The sound to prayer called. It was magical. There wasn't a soul in sight, the sky still dark. There was a café open along the harbour. We sat outside and ordered coffee. Fisherman loaded their boats for the day, a few locals picking up their daily newspaper. The sky lightened and orange coloured the water. The sun rose over the sea, warming our skin. The coffee was strong, the froth golden. We sat there for some time, admiring all. Onur nodded at passers-by and time stood still. There was no talk of what the future may hold, only the promise of the sunrise and life as we know it.

We walked home and I gathered my things. Onur had called a taxi as I said farewell to his family.

'It was lovely to meet you' Ela said softly.

'And you' I replied.

His mother kissed my cheeks and his father bowed his head. Ela gave me the biggest hug and handed me her number. She said she wanted to hear all about life in London. I doubt we'd stay in touch in truth. I'd left her a copy of *Vogue* and the last of my Chanel. It had made her day a year. I took one last look at his home. It was filled with memories, perhaps not the happiest at times, but there was enough love here to last a lifetime.

The taxi parked outside, sounding its horn. Onur loaded my bags into the car and held open the door – always the gentleman. He slid in next to me and I waved goodbye to his family. I rested my head on his shoulder. I was glad he'd agreed to come. He was unsure at first. He said it might be easier if he'd stayed home. Perhaps it would have been but this meant a little longer together. I gazed out of the window as we drove past the harbour. I'd come back one day, I only hoped.

'Rose' he said.

I still loved the way he said my name. I looked at him and he kissed my forehead. There was nothing left to say. We rode in silence, holding one another.

It wasn't long before we arrived at the airport. Onur had asked the driver to wait outside while he helped with my bags. We walked inside the terminal in silence. There was security ahead. This was it, this was goodbye. I turned to face him. There were no words. Time with him had been magical, a dream.

'Thank you for everything' I said, a lump in my throat.

Onur said nothing. I slowly took the ring off my finger and placed it in his palm. It wouldn't be fair to keep it. He should give it to the one he was destined to be with, not the girl passing through town.

'I love you' he said, a tear in his eye.

Tears streamed down my cheeks. He drew breath to speak but I pressed my lips to his. It would be our last until our paths crossed once more – if they ever did that is. I pulled away, my lips now tender.

'Goodbye' I said.

'Rose, this is not goodbye' he whispered, holding me tight.

This time it was goodbye. I let go of him, wiped away the tears and walked away from the man of my dreams. I looked over my shoulder and blew him one last kiss. And just like that, the bubble popped.

I was alone. It was the right thing to do but it felt so wrong. There was a queue for check-in. I thought back to the day I'd left Heathrow for Paris. Gosh, that was a lifetime ago. I'd waved goodbye to the parents and felt like a giddy school girl. The world was my oyster. I had no idea. I'd lived more in the past two weeks than I had my whole life. I

was high on life, high on love. Onur, the sex, the proposal –
it was a dream.

'Ahem' coughed a woman behind.

I came back to reality. I'd day-dreamed for some
time and was now holding up the rest of the queue. I walked
over to the desk, mauling the case. It was heavy.

'Just you?' asked the lady.

It was like taking a bullet. She was chubby with
curly red locks, in her forties and chirpy. She hummed away
as she stamped my passport.

'Please put your case on the scales love' she said,
chuckling to herself.

I knew it'd be over the weight restriction. It had
totted on thirty kilograms flying out and I'd since bought
more. I held my breath. I couldn't bear to part with any of it.

'Nice holiday?' she asked, not noticing that the
scales now read thirty five.

'The best' I beamed.

She typed away on her computer and chatted about
her life here. She'd had a fling with a local bartender and
was in love. No wonder there was a queue. The people were
huffing and puffing behind me. She was sweet but I couldn't
help but judge her a little. It was cliché – a holiday romance.
And it was then that I knew I'd made the right decision.
Then again, she didn't care. She was in love. And she never
did charge me for the extra weight.

I was fed up. I'd looked around duty free at the
overpriced tack and walked past the hordes, in their

hundreds, at the fast-food stalls. Brits in socks and sandals waited for their Big Macs, their children screaming for a Happy Meal. Oh I'd be glad to get home. The plane was delayed a little but I made my way to the gate anyway. I wasn't hungry, I wasn't anything. I felt lost. There were only a few people waiting. It was quiet. I took a seat and exhaled. There was a couple sitting across from me. They were in their fifties, their skin glowing. The man was reading a book and his wife rested her head on his shoulder. They were holding hands. She looked my way and smiled and I couldn't help but smile back.

It had been two hours. Two hours of waiting in a stuffy airport lounge. There weren't enough seats and people were now sitting on the floor. Children ran wild and babies screamed. I'd called Mum and told her I'd be late.

'Don't worry sweetheart. I can't wait to see you' she said.

'You and I both' I replied.

I dreamed of home, toasted crumpets and a cup of tea. I felt warm inside. There really is no place like home.

We spoke for a little while longer, the usual chit-chat. I'd missed her. She said she'd be waiting at the other end for me. I ended the call, my heart full of love for her.

We began boarding. Hundreds of people pushed to the front. It was pointless. The plane wouldn't take off without them. I rolled my eyes and joined the queue.

'Have a nice flight' said the flight attendant as I handed her the boarding pass.

I smiled and took my seat. I was at the front of the plane with a window seat and extra leg room. The woman at check-in must have loved me. I placed my things in the overhead locker and sat down. I looked out of the window at the evening sky. This was my last chance. Was it too late? I'd flee the plane in dramatic fashion and run into Onur's arms once more. I'd say something romantic and we'd live happily ever after with our two children and a golden retriever. I laughed and flicked through the in-flight brochure. Nothing interested me, not even the twenty percent discount. I turned to the drinks. I'd planned to have a cup of tea but the gin list was a better fit. I'd wait until the trolley came round and order copious amounts to drown my sorrows.

'Hello pet'

I looked up to see a plump lady squishing herself into the seat next to me. She was in her late thirties and had a blonde bob.

'I'm Cathy' she said, holding out her hand.

'Rose' I replied.

Truth be told, I wasn't in the mood for small talk. Eleven plane journeys over three months and each one of them was the same. I'd plan the flight – sleep, read *Vogue*, drink wine, read *Vogue* again and sleep some more. It was the perfect plan but every time I'd be sat next to someone who'd just love to chat. Each one as lovely as the next but still, sometimes you just want a little peace and quiet. Cathy was lovely, she was, but she went on and on about the villa with mountain views and an infinity pool. She was here on business.

'It's like I said to my boss, soak up the sun and drink margaritas whilst writing the blog' she said, tittering away.

'It sounds fabulous' I replied, a little sarcastically. I couldn't get a word in edge ways.

I looked out of the window. The plane began to move slowly. Cathy chatted away but I zoned out, her voice muted. I looked at the mountains and the way the sun hit the tarmac. I couldn't breathe and my palms were sweaty. I closed my eyes as my heartbeat quickened. I'd never felt like this before and I couldn't put my finger on what it was. I took a deep breath. The plane was now on the runway. The engines hummed. Cathy passed me a boiled sweet to stop my ears popping. It reminded me of my father. He would always suck on a humbug during take-off. He was a nervous flyer, bless him. The captain said a few words as the engines roared. I took one last look at the view. The sky was dreamy, a deep blue. Tears ran down my face. It was then I knew what I felt. I'd thrown away a chance at love, a chance at life. And just like that, all the magic became a distant dream. Fairy tales are just a myth after all.

Chapter Eighteen

The plane landed with a thud.

'Welcome to Heathrow' announced the captain.

The sky was black and raindrops hit the windows. Home again. We'd hit turbulence mid flight. Cathy held the arm rests, panicking. There was a newborn behind us, she'd cried all the way and children ran up and down the aisle, playing hide and seek with their siblings. I'd fallen asleep for twenty minutes at best. Time didn't seem to pass. I'd munched my way through a pack of salted peanuts and drank two double gin and tonics. Cathy went on about how she'd dated a local a few years back – the best sex of her life – but they'd lost touch. She always hoped that she'd see him again but she never had. I couldn't help but wonder if that's where I'd be in ten years – single and searching for the man

I once loved. And it would be the same story. I'd be a thirty something spinster. I winced at the thought.

We disembarked the aircraft and I said farewell to Cathy. She was heading to Essex for a hen weekend. She squeezed me tightly and went on her way with her leopard print luggage. She was a jolly soul. I hurried through passport control and waited for my suitcase. I'd always fret that someone else would mistake my case for theirs. People were careless. The insurance wouldn't cover the contents of my case. Who pays two hundred pounds for a bikini anyway? And what's more, imagine someone else had your Melissa Odabash two-piece and you were left with an oversized swimsuit on a dream trip away. I waited for some time. It was almost seven and I just wanted to get home. Everyone looked fed up. Families looked weary, children were bored and singletons rolled their eyes. We'd all come back to reality. Oh how I wish I was still in the bubble.

I made my way out of the terminal with my luggage forty minutes later. It was cold and raining. There were no dreamy skies, no sound of crickets in the evening breeze. It was dull, it was lifeless. It was the ordinary life.

'Darling' cried Mum from afar.

I'd hardly seen her before she ran over to me. She held me tightly. She smelt of home and Dior. She'd worn it since I was little. Tears ran down my face and she wiped them away. It didn't matter how old I was, she'd always be there for me.

'I missed you' I sobbed.

'I did more' she said, crying. We were as bad as each other.

Dad kissed my cheek and took my bags. 'Welcome home titch' he said. He was a man of few words but he meant them. I knew he'd missed me.

It was bittersweet. I'd left behind the dream but I was happy to be home. We didn't speak of my mystery man. Mum had told Dad that I'd extended my trip and that was it. He'd only worry. I'd always be his little girl.

The traffic wasn't too bad and we were home in thirty minutes or so. I loved our Kensington town house. The rose bushes were in full bloom. And it was then that I thought of that one red rose – the perfect bud that began our love story.

'Tea?' asked Mum.

I nodded. The house was the same as always, apart from the fresh paint in the hallway.

'It looks fabulous' I said.

Mum shot Dad a look which said *I told you so*. She'd got her own way as usual. Dad turned on the news, popped on his slippers and sat in his favourite chair. He loved being home, like a pig in muck. I went through to the kitchen. Mum had made a cup of Earl Grey in my daffodil Emma Bridgewater mug and toasted crumpets covered with salted butter. I was in heaven. I was a sucker for home comforts.

'So...' said Mum, her eyes widening.

I knew she wanted to know everything. I'd already told her all, well apart from the last chapter that is – Mr.

Tall, Dark and Handsome. It was now or never. I took a deep breath and began the love story, omitting a few details of course. I told her about the rose, dancing under the stars, the sunsets and the love. Once I'd finished my palms were sweaty, my heart racing.

'Wow' she said. 'He sounds, well, perfect.'

He is. He was perfect.

'And he proposed' I added, looking down.

'What?!' she shrieked.

She took hold of my hand, looking for the ring. She'd have loved it, it was a little like hers.

'I said no' I snapped, pulling back my hand.

I knew she wanted to ask why – I'd asked myself that very question – but she didn't.

'Fancy a bath?' she said, her voice bubbly.

I loved her. We both knew we'd talk about it at some point but not now. It was too raw.

'I'd love one' I replied.

I walked into my room. It was just how I'd left it. Pink roses and a welcome home card now lined the dresser. I looked in the mirror. I didn't recognise myself. The tan had already faded, my skin was dull. I looked unhappy and no longer fabulous. I picked up my teddy. I'd had him since as long as I could remember and his fur was now threadbare. I could hear Mum humming in the bathroom. She'd drawn me a bath, bless her. I took off my clothes and fell into the bubbles. The water was hot, soothing my body. Candles twinkled on the windowsill and the smell of lavender filled the room. I felt nothing as I sank into the tub.

'Blow a bubble' shouted Mum through the door.

I said nothing and closed my eyes, sinking deeper into the water. What was the point? There was no magic here.

I'd slept well in the mist of goose down goodness. The sun was shining through the window. Children were playing outside and laughter filled the air. I'd wallowed in my own self pity for the rest of the night but today was a new day. I was better than that. It was late morning. The house was empty. Mum and Dad had already gone to work and it was quite nice to be alone. I made a coffee, strong and black, and sat outside on the patio with toast and damson jam. It was a beautiful day. Now what? I didn't have the heart to unpack or do anything for that matter. I'd just sit here.

I must have sat there for a few hours, alone with my thoughts. Onur, that's all I could think about. Time passed as I stared into space. Rose get up, I told myself. Yes it's sad, but sitting here was only going to make it worse. I got up, got dressed and strolled down to Portobello Road. The market was quieter than usual, still busy nonetheless. I browsed the book stalls, as per usual – still no first editions. I bought some grapes, a baguette and a caramelised onion and Rioja cheddar. I glanced around. People were going about their daily lives. I'd never noticed it before. There may be no harbour, but people sipped coffee and strolled through the markets here too. Sometimes what you're looking for is right in front of you. I sauntered down the road before making my way home.

It was mid afternoon now. Children hopscotched down the streets and people walked their dogs. I sat in the conservatory, the sunlight streaming through the glass. I broke a little bread and gorged on the cheese. I turned on the television and flicked through the channels. *Notting Hill* was on. I'd lost track of how many times I'd seen it. It was amongst my favourites, up there with *Pretty Woman* and *Runaway Bride* – I was a Julia Roberts fan. I snuggled down watching Hugh Grant do what he does best. It was then that it hit me. It was Onur and I. They were worlds apart but Onur was too just a boy, asking a girl to love him – as Julia had said. I turned it off and sat there in silence, staring at the black screen. Hugh had made the wrong decision and so had I. Shit.

I hadn't really moved until my parents came home. What was the point? I'd made a mistake but it was too late now. I wondered what Onur would be doing. He'd probably be on his way back to Istanbul by now. I wanted to call him but our love was over. Our love story had ended.

'Hello sweetheart' beamed Mum.

She'd come back from the office and looked fabulous. She was wearing a tailored white shirt, black midi skirt and courts. She had spent the day filing divorces and I'd just sat here.

'Chinese for dinner?' she asked. I nodded. 'Rose, it'll be okay my love' she said softly, planting a kiss on my forehead.

'I know' I replied.

It would be okay. She'd said the same each time Mark had cheated. It had taken time, and a whirlwind romance but I no longer felt anything for Mark. I just wondered how long it would take to get over Onur.

We'd ordered Chinese – roasted duck in plum sauce and Singapore vermicelli – from the place down the road. It was the comfort food I needed.

'What's the plan kid?' asked Dad. Mum shot him a stern look.

I pushed the noodles around the plate. 'I don't know' I replied.

'You've got all the time in the world sweetheart' said Mum. She had a little more tact.

'Well, I'd love to write' I said.

I'd spoken about writing for years. There's no better time like the present and it would take my mind off things.

'Sounds great' said Dad, tucking into the spare ribs.

Mum tossed around a few ideas – blog posts, travel writing, journalism – but I zoned out a little. I knew what I wanted to write. I'd always wanted to write a novel. I wanted to be up there with The Brontës, Austin and Hardy – the notorious novelists who'd won my heart. I wanted to woe the hearts of the people with a love story. How could I write about the past two weeks? I'd said no. It was a tragic ending but it's not all roses and magic is it? Life as we know it isn't perfect. Once we'd finished dinner, I went up to my room. It was now or never. I'd always put it off. I'd write one word and think it was silly and go back to the mundane life. Not this time.

Two hours had passed and I hadn't written a word, not a single one. I stared at the blank page. I couldn't do it. I couldn't bring myself to relive the magic. It would be better to lock it away, forget it ever happened. No one need know and it was probably better that way. I'd tell myself the story from time to time. Life moves on and that's what I needed to do. Travel writing – that could work.

I'd tried to write about the sights I'd seen but it was all drivel. I give up. I'd go back to the restaurant and live the same life I led before all the magic. Fairy godmothers warn us that magic only lasts so long and then everything goes back to what it was. It was true. I'd been lucky enough to live a little at least.

I looked out of the window. The rain hit the glass, the sky dark once more. It was late August but that's British weather for you. I'd told Eve that I'd see her tomorrow. I couldn't wait to squeeze Susie and have chocolate kisses. I'd catch up with friends and family – I was craving my grandmother's apple pie – and then ask Donatella for my old job. I didn't really have a choice. The writing, if and when it came, wouldn't pay the bills just yet. My parents said they'd help whilst I looked for something but I didn't want to be a Mark. I couldn't live off the wealth of my family. I wanted to make it on my own. I was twenty four; I had little to no savings, no assets and no job. The future wasn't looking so bright. I unpacked my things and looked through my closet. I'd always look at the clothes on a rainy day. It seemed to make things a little better. I put my Manolos to bed – in their shoebox that is – and looked through my jewellery box. I'd inherited a pearl necklace from my late great-grandmother and Mum had given me her diamond and ruby eternity ring for my twenty first. I'd always loved vintage jewellery. How had he known? The ring had been passed down to him but it was like it was meant to be. I wasn't a fan of white gold, I never had been. I loved something with a story, a little history. I glanced down at my left hand. It was like it had never happened. Perhaps it was a dream after all.

I lay on the bed for some time, looking up at the ceiling. *Sex and the City* ran in the background. I flicked through a copy of last year's *Vogue* – even that didn't cheer me up – and I'd eaten half a jar of peanut butter. It would get better. Life would go on. I heard my phone vibrate. It was probably Eve. She'd already called twice since I'd been home. I wasn't in the mood to chat right now. It was eleven thirty and I just wanted to sleep. I declined the call without looking, staring into space. It rang again and I rolled my eyes. I couldn't believe it. It was him. It was Mr. Tall, Dark and Handsome. And just like that, he was no longer a dream.

Chapter Nineteen

"Hello" I answered softly, my heart racing.

'Rose.' He said my name with such love, such tenderness. He rolled his tongue around it as always.

He spoke but I could hardly hear him. The line crackled. His voice was barely audible.

'Onur' I said his name over and over.

The line went dead. He was gone. And just like that, the light faded once more. This is what life would be like. Thousands of miles apart, divided by the seas, we'd hold onto each phone call. That's if we could actually hear one other. I wanted him day in and day out, not once every few months for a fleeting week of passion. That's not the relationship I wanted. I'd have to move abroad to be with him to make this work. Was I ready for that? What's more, is that what I wanted? What did he want? Why had he called? We both knew it was over. It's not like we could be friends. We had nothing in common. Our love was based on attraction – a fatal one. I let myself fall head over heels for someone I knew was unattainable. I'd listened to my heart. I always knew it would end in tears but I just couldn't say no. The phone beeped. This time it was a message:

'I miss you.'

Three words, nothing more but they meant so much. He could have moved on to the next girl by now. He was a dreamboat and could have anyone he wanted yet he still chose me. I longed for him. I too missed him, his touch and the way he held me. I'd opened my heart to him. I began to reply, declaring my love but then deleted the words. What was I doing? I loved him but it was over and we both needed to face it. We both needed to move on. I needed to forget him. I closed the phone and shut my eyes tightly, holding back the tears. It was the right thing to do.

I'd lay awake for most of the night. It was no surprise that I couldn't sleep. I tossed and turned, gazing out of the open window. I wondered if he too was looking at the sky, the stars which we'd danced beneath. It was possible and romantic. I'd tell myself to shut up and went back to counting sheep – it didn't work. I promised I'd see Eve today. She'd invited me round for a cheese and wine night so I couldn't refuse.

'Auntie Rose!' Susie screamed as I walked through the door.

I scooped her up and kissed her all over. She still had that baby smell which I adored. She was wearing a Cinderella dress and had chocolate in her hair. I'd missed her. She made life that little bit brighter. She tootled off to the kitchen with her plastic wand, humming as she went.

Eve gave me the biggest hug. 'Welcome home babe' she said, a little teary.

It was then that I realised I'd never truly be alone. I may not have my Prince Charming but I was loved and that made up for the happy ever after – for now anyway.

Eve put Susie to bed. H, her husband, took himself upstairs with *Star Wars* and a couple of beers. He said he'd give us girls some alone time but I think he was secretly happy in his own company. He was the perfect guy. He was an accountant, handsome and loved Eve more than she knew. And what's more, he was a wonderful father to Susie. He adored her.

Eve had bought every type of cheese known to man, chutney, fresh bread and a bottle of red. She said there was more in the garage and I think we'd need it. *Bridget Jones's Diary* was playing in the background.

'Tell me everything' she said.

I went on about the sights, the countries I'd visited.

'Tell me about him, Mr. Right' she said.

I took a deep breath. I had to tell her. I couldn't keep this from her and I didn't want to. She'd been a lifesaver during the Mark fiasco. She was the one who said I should get away and clear my head.

'Are you sitting comfortably?' I asked, gulping the wine.

She nodded, her eyes widening

I told her everything, every sordid detail. I told her about the sex, the romance and finally, the proposal.

'What?!' she screamed.

I'm surprised she didn't wake Susie.

'What?' she repeated, this time lowering her voice.

I twisted the end of my hair and blushed.

'Rose, did you say yes?' she asked, raising her brows.

'Not in the end' I replied.

'And what does that mean?' she asked, frowning.

I told her about the drunken answer, the dreamy picnic and the perfect ring. I relived the magic once more. She was speechless. She said it sounded like something from a novel – if only I could write about it – and then asked the dreaded question.

'Why?' she asked.

It was the question I'd asked myself a hundred times over. Why did I give back the ring? Why did I leave? Why did I say no to love?

'I don't know' I replied. It was the truth. I didn't know why. 'It wouldn't have worked.'

Eve shrugged. That's what I loved about her. She took everything with a pinch of salt. There may not be rhyme or reason to life but she'd see the light in everything. Well, apart from Mark. She hated him after he broke my heart. She only ever wanted me to be happy and Sophie – the other blonde – was the last straw. Onur was different. She said he sounded dreamy and that he was. She said that it was a risk but that I should listen to my heart.

'You only live once Ro' she said.

Maybe she was right. Time would tell. I lightened the mood and spoke about the sex, the incredible mind-blowing sex, for some time. She and H had managed to sneak a five minute tussle in the sheets the other night before Susie walked in on them. She wanted to play hide and seek too. Eve rolled her eyes.

'I've got all that to look forward to' I said, laughing.

'Enjoy the hot sex while you can' she replied, knocking back the wine. 'Another bottle?' she asked.

'Sure' I said.

We watched the rest of *Bridget Jones's Diary* – she's a thirty something spinster and still gets her happy ending. There is hope yet. We ate our way through the cheese and guzzled the wine, giggling through the night. Laughter really is the best medicine. And you can't get through anything without your friends.

Eve let me stay the night. I slept right through, no star gazing or counting sheep. It was probably down to the fact that we'd drunk three bottles of wine and on a school night as well – not that that mattered anymore. It still felt like we were fifteen at times.

'Auntie Rose!' Susie screamed.

She jumped on me, pulling my hair and piling her teddies on top of me. I tickled her and she laughed hysterically.

H rushed out to the office. He'd had one too many beers last night by the looks of it. He waved hello, grabbed a slice of toast and kissed his girls goodbye. Eve was still in her dressing gown and looked a little fragile. She put *Beauty and the Beast* on for Susie and made smashed avocado and poached eggs for us. We chatted over breakfast and Susie hummed along to *'Be Our Guest',* having a tea party of her own with her teddies. I stayed until the afternoon. I had nothing to rush home for. We painted pretty pictures and baked cupcakes. Life with a child was manic and anything but boring. I walked home a little later and finally felt like myself. I was thankful to have them in my life. Eve was right, a Disney film and baking makes everything better.

The next few days were a bit of a blur. I met up with Ivy the next afternoon for lunch in Chelsea. There was a new sushi bar that, according to her, we just had to try. I had yellowfin tuna nigiri and it was amazing. I told her about the dream trip – apart from the last chapter that is. I couldn't bring myself to mention Onur. No one else need know. I needed to forget him. Ivy told me how she and Ted were giving it another go. They had seen each other at an art show a few weeks back and he looked better than ever. They kissed and he moved back in the next day. It didn't surprise me. They were childhood sweethearts and could finish each other's sentences.

'It was his bloody mother's fault' she began, cursing Hilda. I knew it.

'What about you?' she asked after some time.

I shook my head.

'You'll find him Ro. He's out there' she said hopefully.

'Maybe' I replied, shrugging.

Perhaps I would, maybe I wouldn't. That was the risk I had to take.

We took a taxi to Covent Garden mid afternoon. Ivy didn't have any other plans, it was her day off, and nor did I. She worked at *Elle* – not quite *Vogue* but still. She kept me updated on the latest fashion scandals, along with this season's it bag. Her life was like a glossy magazine. She was fabulous and she knew it. She and Ted didn't want children. They were happy with their lives. Who wouldn't be? They were rich, lived in a beautiful townhouse in the city and knew The Beckhams. I'd swap lives with her. We browsed the market. There was nothing worth looking at and Ivy wasn't a fan of the second hand stalls. We took a seat outside at a bar in the midst of the square under the sun.

'Champagne please' she said to the waiter. He nodded.

'Ivy' I said sternly.

She raised her hand 'Don't Ro. We're celebrating.'

I'd known her since we were little. Our parents were – well are – good friends and we followed in their footsteps. I'd always admired her. She spoke her mind and was a loyal friend. The waiter placed a bottle of Veuve on ice, popping the cork and filling our flutes.

'Welcome home' she said as we clinked our glasses together.

'He's hot' she whispered as the waiter left.

He was and I couldn't blame her for trying. She'd tried to set me up with Ted's bachelor friends after Mark and I had spilt. She said it would take my mind of him. Ted had some attractive, and very wealthy, friends but I'd always say no to the blind dates. I was an old-school romantic. Ivy went on about her mother-in-law – monster-in-law more like – as we sipped the fizz and watched the performers in the square.

We shared a taxi home. Ivy only lived two streets over. It was dusk and we had since made our way through two bottles of Veuve – her treat. It was a lovely afternoon, just what I needed to take my mind off things.

'Come over for dinner next week' she said, hugging me. 'And remember, you're fabulous.' It was her favourite word – very Carrie Bradshaw.

'As are you' I said, blowing her a kiss as she got out of the cab.

I rode the next two streets smiling, full on fizz and talk of couture.

I sat in my room, a little tipsy. I looked at the blank page. Come on Rose, you can do this. Truth is, I wasn't sure if I wanted to. I still hadn't replied to Onur's message and I don't think I was going to either. What would I say? It was better this way. I spent the night eating my way through a jar of peanut butter and flicking through my stack of *Vogue*. This is how I dealt with break-ups. I'd over indulge and loose myself in the fashion. And I couldn't think of a better way. The writing could wait. Life could wait.

I stood in front of the mirror the following morning and practised my speech. I sounded pathetic. I was pathetic. I'd had all these dreams but here I was, pleading for my old job back. Who knew how long it would be before the writing came, if it ever did. And I needed to fund my current wine and peanut butter addiction. I would wait tables for a little longer before I got back on my feet. Who was I kidding? I'd probably still be there by the end of the year. I looked at my reflection. I felt more lost than ever. And this wasn't about Onur. I didn't know what to do next, where to go. I'd drift through life and before I know it, life would flash before me. I'd miss my chance at living. I took a deep breath and said the speech once more.

Donatella was just how I'd remembered. She was a large lady, in her mid sixties, with dark hair and red lips. She ran the Italian with her husband, Gio. It was quaint with red and white checked tablecloths, oil lamps and bread baskets. I had to admit, I'd loved working there. I'd met some lovely people over the years. Frank read his newspaper and had his morning tipple – Limoncello – every day at eleven thirty. We didn't open until midday but he'd become an exception. And then there was the old lady who had a glass of red in the afternoon after walking her French bulldog. She was a sweetheart.

'I told you, didn't I?' Donatella said smugly, her hands on her hips.

She had told me. I never thought I'd be stood here but here I was. I was begging for a job that I didn't even want. She said I could have three shifts a week. It was enough for now and it would give me time to write. I thanked her and we made small talk for the best part of two minutes before I went on my way. She wasn't all bad. Life did go on. It wasn't where I saw myself but it was a stop gap – I'd been saying that for years – and I would find what I was looking for one day.

It was another lovely day. I walked for a while. London had a buzz like no other. There were no mountain goats, no dreamy sunsets or fishing boats here. The city was home but did I see myself here in ten years time? I couldn't say. It was a Thursday afternoon. I smiled at the passers-by but they were too busy with their daily lives to notice. Life here wasn't relaxed. People rushed to work with their Starbucks, others jogging through the streets. Traffic blocked the roads and cyclists sped past. I was a city girl but there was no harm dreaming of the coast, was there?

I'd walked for some time. I thought I'd visit my grandparents. They lived in Notting Hill. I knocked on the door and my grandmother held me tightly.

'Rose!' She cried.

We all sat at the kitchen table, chatting away. I told the tales, the magical stories of my trip. They had never been abroad. They'd lived here all their lives.

'Oh sweetheart, it sounds wonderful' she said, her eyes sparkling.

There was an apple pie on the table. She must have sensed I'd visit. She put on a pot of tea and cut me a slice of pie. It tasted just like home. Gran told me about the latest rumours of the street – she was a gossip – and Grandad held her hand. They'd been married for close to sixty years and were still madly in love. Photographs lined the mantelpiece, telling the story of their lives together.

'What's next?' she asked, drinking her tea.

I placed the china teacup down. She always used her fine china for company.

'I don't know' I replied.

'As long as you're happy my dear' she said.

Grandad pottered in the garden shortly after to prune the roses and check on his tomatoes. He loved gardening, it was his calm. He had retired twenty years ago now and this got him through the days. Gran would spend her afternoons reading her love stories outside and drinking tea. They led a simple life but they were happy. Gran and I sat on the porch whilst Grandad fussed over his strawberries. She poured us a glass of brandy. I can't say I was a fan but why not.

'Are you happy?' she asked.

I couldn't reply. I'd had the dream childhood and everything I'd ever wanted. I was happy. But was I happy right now? Everyone had moved on with their lives and I was stuck in limbo. I was twenty four and still clueless. I looked down and took another sip.

'Listen sweetheart, don't rush into things. You have your whole life ahead of you and only your heart knows what it wants. Grandad and I will always be here for you.'

She was the sweetest. She'd always believed in true love and fate. And she was right. It all meant nothing if I wasn't happy.

'Listen to your heart' she said. And that's exactly what I needed to do.

That evening I lay on my bed and gazed out of the open window. It was still light outside, the sky pink across the rooftops. The moon was out and bigger than ever. Onur and I were over. Perhaps it was the end of our love story but I couldn't help but think that Onur too was looking at the moon, just as I. He and I were dancing under the stars once more. That's what my heart told me anyway.

Chapter Twenty

I'd been home for three weeks now. Time passed by and I was still none the wiser. I had written all of fifty words of drivel and made my way through six jars of crunchy peanut butter. Life was anything but fabulous. The trip of dreams was a lifetime ago. I never had replied to Onur. I wanted to but I couldn't. There had been no more messages, no phone calls. There wasn't a day that went by that I didn't think of him. I relived the magic and danced under the stars and I hoped he did too. We were over but I'd never forget him.

The restaurant was busy as always. The days were still warm, the evenings cool. Donatella and Gio had gone to Italy for the weekend and had given the keys to me. I'd open up mid morning and lock the doors in the evening. I'd be living here for the next few days by the sounds of it. I didn't mind. It took my mind off things and they said they'd bring me home some Gorgonzola. We were short staffed and the newbies were already testing my patience.

'Katie' I sighed for the hundredth time.

'What?' She rolled her eyes.

She was seventeen and this was her first job. She'd only been here a week. She had long acrylic nails, the shortest skirt I'd ever seen and an attitude. She didn't want to be here – nor did any of us for that matter.

'I've told you to tie your hair back' I said.

She flicked her brown locks over her shoulder and rolled her eyes again. She was pretty, that went without saying but she knew it.

'Now' I said sternly.

She sighed, twisted the curls into a ponytail and went back to polishing cutlery, muttering under her breath. She spent the next hour flirting with Luca, the Italian sous-chef. I give up.

I wasn't sure if I'd make it through the weekend. Ben couldn't pronounce half the dishes on the menu – he'd asked if Tiramisu was a drink. Josh had munched his way through half of the breadsticks and Tim had sliced his hand open grating parmesan. I made my way around the tables, pouring wine and chatting with the guests. Everyone was happy, full on Chianti and beef ragu. I wasn't quite sure how I'd pulled it off but I had. It was eleven once everyone had left. I kicked off my shoes and cooked the books. Antonio had made me a little fettuccine before he headed home. He was Gio's cousin and a sweetheart. I'd always been fond of him. He was good looking but in his forties and a tad overweight.

'*Ciao bella*' he said as he left.

I poured myself a glass of red and sighed. It had been a long day.

It was gone midnight by the time I'd finished. It was raining and cold. I stood beneath the canopy, looking into the night sky. The stars were hidden behind the clouds. There was no one around and no taxis in sight. The rain bounced off the footpath as I walked home. I wasn't looking where I was going and bumped into someone walking the other way.

'I'm sorry' I said.

'Rose, is that you?' the man asked.

I looked up. It was him. He was handsome, more so than ever. He brushed back his wet hair and smiled. I was speechless, my heart racing. Was it really him? It was. It was Mark.

'Come on' he said, pulling me to one side out of the rain.

He always wormed his way back into my life one way or the other.

'How are you?' he asked, kissing my cheek.

I wanted to run. I was drenched and had never looked worse. 'I'm okay' I replied.

I should have said that I was fabulous and walked on, giving him the finger as I went. I was anything but fabulous right now. I'd gone over what I'd say to him a thousand times if I ever saw him again. And it wasn't anything like this.

'You look...well' he said.

He was lying. I looked awful and he, well he'd never looked better. He wore a tailored suit, a red tie and brown dress shoes. He carried his briefcase in one hand, an umbrella in the other. He was a business man through and through. He looked grown up, he looked different.

'So you're back?' he asked.

He was making small talk and Mark never made small talk. I nodded. I didn't know what to say to him. There were no words left.

'I've got to run. Fancy dinner next week?' he asked as if nothing had happened between us.

Was he kidding? Did he really think I'd say yes?

'Mark' even saying his name hurt. 'I don't think that's a good idea' I said. He knew this as much as I did.

'If you change your mind' he said, handing me his business card. 'It was good to see you Rose.' He kissed my cheek once more and walked on.

I stood in the rain, mascara running down my face. It had been six months since I'd seen him and just like that, he'd come back into my life. I didn't know what to feel. He looked incredible and was anything but smug. I shook my head and walked on. The universe was really screwing with me. And with that I tore up the card and threw it in my bag.

Two days passed and I played the moment over and over. Was it a sign? Perhaps it was fate that we'd bumped into each other. Maybe it was another chance at love.

'Rose, don't you dare!' Eve shouted. 'You are not going on a date with him. He broke your heart.'

'I don't think the guy at the back heard you' I said, sarcastically.

I'd asked Eve to meet me for coffee. I didn't know what to do. Everything happens for a reason and maybe this had too.

'He looked different' I said.

She rolled her eyes. 'This is Mark we're talking about. You and I both know how that dinner will end.'

Of course I knew. He'd wine and dine me, we'd go back to his apartment and have sex – not mind-blowing either – and then he wouldn't call me for weeks. I'd spend the next month eating peanut butter and drinking wine – I was already doing that but still.

'Please Ro' she said softly. 'I don't want you getting hurt again.'

She was right. It was a risk and we both knew how it would end. I'd wasted years of my life chasing Mark and it had always ended in tears. I nodded and took a sip of the pumpkin spiced latte. I still couldn't believe it was October.

'Ro, I've got to run. I've got to pick Susie up from nursery' she said, gathering her things. 'Remember, you're worth a hundred of him.' She blew me a kiss and hurried out.

I sat there for some time. The coffee shop was filled with mothers and their babies, elderly couples and singletons, some pretentious and others simply passing the day. I ordered a cinnamon bagel and another latte. There was no rush. I pulled out my notepad and looked over the words I'd written. The novelists of the nineteenth century would turn in their graves. I put a line through the nonsense. The writing will come. Who was I kidding? I'd spent weeks staring at a blank page and still nothing. I was flogging my guts at a restaurant with no savings, no relationship and no hope. I may as well give up now.

I read *Hello!* and caught up on the dresses of Paris Fashion Week and inside Sarah Jessica Parker's Manhattan home. It was a miserable day but a little fashion news made it that little bit brighter. I scanned over the horoscopes. I wasn't sure if I believed in zodiac signs but I'd always read mine anyway. *'Full moons serve a purpose this month...'* it began. I rolled my eyes. *'Not all is out of your reach and fate is on your side this week'* – nothing but hocus-pocus.

I walked home once the rain had stopped and couldn't help but wonder if there was more to it. Perhaps fate was on my side. Maybe I should go. It's only dinner after all.

I salvaged the torn business card from my tote and called Mark the next day.

'This is a surprise' he said.

Is it too late to hang up? Hang up Rose.

'I was thinking, maybe we should go for that dinner' I said, cringing.

He paused, taken a back. 'Great' he replied.

I was half expecting him to make some cheesy innuendo but he didn't. Maybe he had changed.

'When works for you?' he asked.

'Friday?'

'It's a date' he said.

No, no, no. It was not a date. I was not dating Mark. This was just a friendly dinner for old times' sake. Now this would be the time to hang up but I didn't.

'I'll pick you up at eight on Friday then' he said.

'Cool' I replied and ended the call. Cool? Oh fabulous. I was pathetic.

I spent the next few hours squirming at the phone call. Could I have sounded any more desperate? He'd broken my heart, more than once, and I was going for dinner with him. This wasn't just anyone. This was Mark. I sighed and ate my way through another jar of peanut butter and binge watched *Sex and the City*. I needed some glamour in my life right now.

Donatella and Gio were back from their trip. They'd brought me back the cheese, as promised, and some Amaretto. I wasn't a fan but Dad would love it. We'd had some fabulous reviews this weekend so I was a little smug. I'd told Donatella about Katie and she sighed. I didn't envy her. The weekend had been tough and she did this week in, week out. Gio wrote today's specials on the chalkboard and Antonio baked rosemary focaccia. The smell was unreal. The day dragged and it was quieter than usual. I'd drunk three espressos since we'd opened. Gio went on about Sicily. He said the sun set over the blue seas and they drank wine from the local vineyard. And just like that, I longed for pink skies and dreamy seas once more.

'Would it be okay if I take tomorrow off?' I'd been plucking up the courage to ask all day.

'Why?' asked Donatella.

'Well, I've kind of got a date' I said, stuttering.

She raised her brows. Was it really that surprising that I had a date? It probably was.

'Go on then' she said. 'Antonio won't be happy.'

Antonio flared red and went back to baking his bread. It was no secret that he had a little crush on me. He was a darling but no, just no. He was almost twice my age. I had a skip in my step for the rest of the day.

Mark said we'd have a drink at The Ritz – very fancy – and then on to dinner. I'd spent the day musing what I should wear. I'd changed at least eight times. Mum gave me the filthiest look when I said I was going out with Mark. I said it was just a friendly dinner but she reminded me that *friendly* wasn't in Mark's vocabulary. It was seven thirty and I was still standing in my underwear. I wanted to look hot. I wanted him to see what he'd lost, what he was missing. It's just dinner, this is not a date. I repeated that over and over.

I wore a black satin backless dress, a red lip and Manolos. I looked fabulous. The doorbell rang and it felt like prom night all over again. I took a deep breath and opened the door. He looked good, too good. He was wearing a black suit, white shirt and pearl cufflinks. He took my hand and kissed it in true gentleman style. He had changed.

'You look stunning' he said. I blushed. 'Shall we?' he asked.

I took his hand and stepped outside.

'I'm so happy we're doing this Rose' he said.

I smiled. I had to admit, so was I. It was a risk but you only get one shot at life. We walked down the road to his car. The Bentley belonged to his late grandfather – another thing he'd inherited. He held open the door and I slid onto the leather seats. He sped down the street, wind rushing through the open windows. I felt alive. And just like that, I was twenty again without a care in the world.

Chapter Twenty One

We made it to The Ritz in one piece. Mark tossed the keys to the doorman.

'Very well Sir' he said, nodding his head towards us.

I'd never been here – well apart from in the movies. It was stunning. Chandeliers lit the carpeted hallways and a grand piano stood on the black and white tiled floor. Everyone looked elegant. Women wore pearls, the men in black tie. The place exuded affluence and I felt fabulous. The maitre d' escorted us the cocktail lounge. Mark had requested a booth and a bottle of Dom Pérignon on ice. There was a champagne and caviar list on the marble table – of course there was. The waiter filled our flutes with the three hundred pound fizz and we clinked our crystal glasses together.

'Cheers' he said.

I took a sip. The almond aroma lingered on my tongue, the bubbles ending in floral notes. I'd taken a wine tasting class a few years back and it was worth every penny. I too could swirl wine and compliment its character and body. Mark took a gulp. He'd always been pretentious. He would order something because it was the most expensive, not necessarily the best. I had to admit, Dom was the Da Vinci of champagnes – I couldn't argue with that.

'I'm a little surprised you're here' said Mark.

Truth be told, so was I. This was Mark. Mark and I were on a date, drinking champagne as if nothing had happened. I didn't reply.

'So, how are you?' he asked.

'Fabulous' I replied, flicking my hair.

'I can see that' he said, winking.

He was always the flirt. He had that twinkle in this eye.

'How was your trip?' he asked.

I'd never told him that I was going away. I'd broken things off, once and for all, and booked the ticket the next day. H was a friend of Marks' – well not a friend per se but they had the same group of friends – much to Eve's dismay. She'd even turned down an all-expenses-paid trip to New York because Mark would be there. H went alone and Eve and I spent the weekend drinking wine and burning photos of Mark and me – memories. I had to move on. That was six months ago and he'd changed. I went on about the trip of dreams – skipping over my whirlwind romance – for some time. Mark listened. He would always go on and on about his life but not this time. He was actually listening and seemed interested in what I had to say. We spoke of the past and the future and time ticked by. We'd since made our way through the champagne and he'd ordered a cosmopolitan for me and a double Macallan – twenty five years old and over two hundred pounds a shot – for him. Money was just no object for him. The cosmopolitan was delicious, the best I'd tasted. Mark swirled his finger along the rim of the glass. He didn't take his eyes off me. I blushed.

'Hungry?' he asked.

'Starving' I replied.

He smirked. Shit. How had I forgotten? This had always been our code for sex. He'd ask if I was hungry – for him quite literally – and we'd go back to his.

'I've got a reservation at The Savoy' he then said, winking.

I blushed again. He laughed and downed his drink. Perhaps he had changed.

'Ready?' he asked.

I nodded. I'd only had a few sips of the thirty pound cocktail but I'd already had three glasses of champagne. I couldn't be drunk, not tonight. And I didn't want to say yes to another proposal any time soon either. Not that Mark would probably ever settle down that is.

Mark held out his hand for mine and we made our way to the lobby. I almost broke my neck watching The Beckhams pass by. I felt like I knew them, I didn't but I lived vicariously through Ivy. I couldn't fault the evening. Mark had wined and dined me in true gentleman style. He wasn't obnoxious or crude. He had changed. I began to wonder if he'd ever been as bad as I made out. He had cheated on me but did that fuel the hatred? There was a time that I was head over heels in love with this man. Perhaps it was fate that brought us back together. Everyone does deserve a second chance.

Mark and I had dined at The Savoy last year for our anniversary. I'd found out about Sophie the following week and the world had ended as I knew it. The wonderful memories of our dream date, and life together, faded. I just couldn't budge the image of them at it like rabbits. That was a long time ago Rose. I'd like to think that we'd both grown up since then.

It was just how I'd remembered. The dining room had wooden interior and brass chandeliers. The tables were adorned with linen cloth, crystal glassware and fragrant candles. I recalled our decadent three course meal. I was starving and couldn't wait. I'd order anything and everything I wanted. He owed me that at least. Mark ordered a bottle of Côtes du Rhône and a dozen oysters to start. He ordered for me – he'd always done so and I hated it. I kind of thought this time would be different. We weren't dating, we were two friends. He didn't own me, not anymore. I had to admit, the smoked loin of venison sounded unreal but I'd have gone for the duck. I didn't say anything and smiled. I guess not all things change.

The waiter poured the wine. I took great pleasure in swirling it around the glass and licking my lips together. I nodded and he filled our glasses.

'To us' Mark said, holding up his glass.

I smiled. I couldn't bring myself to do the same. Perhaps this was fate but it wouldn't just take a fancy dinner to make everything right again. He'd hurt me. He'd broken my heart.

The oysters came in a flash and Mark put the first one to my lips. I can't say I saw the obsession. He had always ordered them – pretentious as ever – but I quite fancied the parfait.

'They're an aphrodisiac' he whispered, winking.

He had said this each time we'd had them. The first time I went weak at the knees but come the fourth time it got old. And he was still doing it now. I wondered how many women he'd said this to.

I hadn't said much. Mark spoke of how well business was doing – more like how much he was earning. He bragged about his new penthouse apartment in the city and his time share in Rio. It sounded dreamy but I was anything but interested. He'd spent the last forty five minutes in awe of himself. I even caught him looking at his reflection in the silverware. I thanked god when our main course arrived. The waiter placed the napkin in my lap and poured a little more wine. He spilled a drop on the white linen. I glanced at Mark. He was staring at the red stain.

'Do you know how much that costs?' he said sternly.

'My apologies Sir' stammered the waiter.

'More than you make in a week' Mark added.

The young boy lowered his head and hurried away. Classic Mark I thought. We didn't speak. He cut through the meat, sighing.

'What's wrong?' I asked.

'It should be pink' he answered, anger in his voice.

'It's pinkish' I said.

The dish looked incredible. I couldn't see the problem.

'It's not right' he shot back.

He clicked his fingers and a waitress came across. I'd told Mark over and over not to do that. He knew I worked as a waitress yet he did it all the more. It was belittling.

'Yes Sir' she said politely. I knew she'd be cursing him deep down.

'This should be pink' he said, raising his voice.

The couple at the next table looked over.

'I am not happy in the slightest. This is incompetence!' He yelled.

It was embarrassing, that's what this was. He was making a scene – for no reason other than he could – and everyone was looking. I was mortified. I placed my hand over his.

'It's fine' I said softly.

'You don't know what you're talking about' he snapped back.

The woman at the next table raised her brows. She was most likely thinking what an arsehole he was or why an earth I was with him. I was thinking the same thing. The waitress apologised once more and took the dishes away. He hadn't changed. He was exactly how I'd remembered, perhaps worse.

I excused myself to go to the ladies. I needed to get away. I sat on the chaise longue in the midst of the marble bathroom and took a deep breath. How could I have been so stupid? I was right back at square one. I knew this would happen but I kept lying to myself that things would be different this time. Things weren't different. I splashed a little water on my face, holding back the tears and ran the red across my lips. I could go back and live a lie or I could go and live my life. It wasn't fate. Mark and I were over, more so than ever. And I finally got it. I wanted a life filled with love, not with luxury. I wanted a man who loved me, not loved the idea of me. I wanted him, I wanted Onur. I looked down at my Manolos. The jewelled buckle twinkled in the lights. I clicked them together just like Dorothy and whispered *"There's no place like home"*. I wanted to be in the Land of Oz once more. Things aren't quite that simple in real life. If only I had a pair of ruby slippers.

I looked at myself for some time. I wasn't fabulous. I must have been gone twenty minutes by now. I'd like to think Mark would be wondering where I was but he'd probably be on a business call or flirting with the hot maitre d'. I couldn't do this. I had to leave. I debated making a run for it and leaving him alone with his overcooked venison but I didn't. I was the better person. I made my way over to the table. He sat there, drumming his fingers impatiently on the table cloth. He looked at me, straight-faced. I couldn't even tell what he was thinking but deep down I knew. He loved to win and this was a chance to win me back, even if just for the night. I'd left him and he couldn't stand to lose. I was a pawn in his game of chess and I wasn't willing to play anymore.

'I'm leaving' I said.

He looked at me and said nothing. He didn't fight for me or declare his love. He was the same old Mark.

'No loss' he said, looking ahead. 'Sophie is stopping by later.' He smirked. He knew it would hurt and it did.

I wanted to scream. I hated him. And then I did something which I should have done a long time ago. I picked up the overpriced wine, took a sip and threw the rest over him. He gasped.

'Rose!' He shouted.

The woman at the next table applauded and the waiter smiled at me.

'Get me a towel, NOW!' He yelled at the waitress.

I turned on my heel and had never felt more fabulous. Perhaps I did have a pair of ruby slippers after all. I wasn't stuck in Kansas anymore. I was finally free.

I stepped outside and laughed. The doorman hailed me a cab.

'What the hell were you thinking?' yelled Mark, chasing after me.

His white shirt was stained red. He was furious and I was smug – for once. I had nothing to say to him. It was over.

'Do you know what you're missing?' he shouted.

He was full of himself. He thought the world began and ended with him but I'd realised that there is so much more to life than money and looks. I did know what I was missing. I said nothing and got into the taxi. He stood on the side of the road, humiliated.

I smiled all the way home. Eve was right, it was a mistake but it was something I had to do. I finally had closure. It was the first time in months that I'd felt driven. I wanted to live again. I wanted to write. I wanted Onur. I dialled his number, my heart racing. I stopped. How could I? What would I say? I broke his heart. And just like that, the magic ended and everything was as it was in true fairy-tale style.

Chapter Twenty Two

'How was it?' Mum asked over coffee the next morning.

I smirked as my inner goddess high-fived me. I still couldn't believe I'd done it. I'd given Mark a taste of his own medicine and ruined his Prada shirt in doing so.

'Eventful' I replied.

Mum raised her brows a little. She wanted to know all, even I knew that. Dad was pottering in the garden, planting the hydrangea she'd asked him to. Mum had been hanging around the kitchen all morning. She'd even missed her sunrise yoga class – something she never missed.

'Give me something Ro' she snapped after a minute or so. And I told her all.

She let out the loudest laugh. 'He deserved it sweetheart, after everything he put you through. What a prick.'

I couldn't agree more. We chatted all morning, just like old times. Dad stayed out of the way and Mum made margaritas come midday. We sat in the conservatory, the autumn light streaming through the glass. I'd missed this.

'So, what about a certain someone else?' she asked after her second refill.

I sighed. I still hadn't spoken to Onur. I wanted to but how could I?

'It's complicated' I replied.

'Love is always complicated' she said, licking the salt off the rim of her glass. 'Do what your heart tells you sweetheart.'

My heart was telling me to run away into the sunset, find my dreamboat and live happily ever after but that's just silly isn't it?

I'd had three margaritas by mid afternoon and felt a little sloshed. I had drunk more these past few months than ever but luckily I'd curbed my peanut butter addiction which my thighs were thankful for. I loved spending time with Mum but it was a rarity. The weekends were always the same story. Her mornings were taken up with yoga and treatments and her afternoons were spent working on briefs and confirming appointments for the week ahead. Sundays had always been our day. We'd play hopscotch, bake cakes and watch Cinderella when I was a little girl. There were picnics in the park, pyjama days and horse riding lessons. I lived for these days together but they became sporadic over time. I'd grown up and life moves on. I'd spend the weekends with

Mark. How silly had I been? I'd spent less and less time with the light of my life for some crummy man. It was time I'd never get back. Now was the time to set that right.

'Fancy another?' I asked, already filling her glass.

'You know me too well' she replied.

We'd made our way through half a bottle of tequila. I can't say I was the biggest fan of margaritas so I switched to wine after the fourth glass. We watched *The Notebook* and sobbed our hearts out. And then I got it. The great love stories are about the impossible relationship – girl falls head over heels for the man she shouldn't or can't be with. It may be fiction but that's what pulls on your heart strings. Perhaps I should write about our love, the love story across the seas, after all.

It was gone eight. We'd binged watched much-loved romantic films, drank copious amounts and devoured a cheese fondue and a tub of ice-cream. It was the perfect day and exactly what I'd needed. Mum had since fallen asleep on the sofa and I made my way up to bed. I was tipsy – very tipsy actually. I glanced at the blank page on the desk. I'd wasted weeks mulling over what I should write but I'd known all along. I scribbled the words on the page and fell into the deepest of sleeps.

I woke with a headache like no other. I pulled the duvet over my head, blocking out the outside noises. I felt dreadful. I stumbled to the bathroom and splashed cold water over my face. Those margaritas were not a good idea. I should know by now that tequila wasn't my friend. I tied my hair into a messy bun, brushed my teeth and pulled on an oversized t-shirt. I may not be a little girl anymore but today was a pyjama day – there was no question about that. I staggered back into my room and took a deep breath. It was just after ten. I couldn't remember when I'd slept this well – when there wasn't an orgasm involved that is. I looked at my phone but still nothing. What was I hoping for? I guess I hoped that Onur would declare his love for me. He had, more than once. And what had I done? I was the girl who'd broken his heart. I threw it down and looked at the writing on the page.

'In any language, it's you I love'

It was a drunken scrawl but couldn't be closer to the truth. And just like that, I was one step closer to the dream.

I spent the day drinking tea, eating bacon sandwiches and watching re-runs of *Sex and the City*. Mum looked fragile but she had a brief to work on. Dad read his newspaper, pruned his flowers and had a conference call with the Swizz late afternoon. The day flew by and all I could think of was what I'd written. It was true. I loved him in ways I couldn't even imagine. He was the man in my love story. It may not be real but I could relive it once more.

The next day I wrote three pages, painting the picture of where we fell in love. It took me right back to the magic, our whirlwind romance. This was it. I looked out of the window and daydreamed a little. The sky was cloudy. Perhaps I'd write this and one day Onur would read it, come running back to me and we would live happily ever after. It would be a romantic classic in itself and Austin would be proud. I'd managed to write several pages by the end of the day. It was happening. I was doing what I'd always dreamed of. I couldn't help but feel a little smug. I'd tell Donatella that she could stick her job as I was a published author – not quite yet but one can dream.

Life at the restaurant was easy after that. I'd spend the days serving carbonara and the evenings writing the love story. I found that hours would pass as I'd lose myself in the moment. There was no more wine – except the occasional glass of course – or peanut butter. Months passed and I'd written almost half the book. I felt alive. I had a purpose. I'd embellished the story slightly but I still couldn't believe that I'd lived this life. I was the girl I was writing about and she was, well, fabulous. I'd written about the rose, the romance and the passion. I was hooked on a story I knew inside and out and still wanted to know more. Then, reality hit. There was no more romance. I'd soon come to the end of the magic and how would I finish? There was no twist. The girl hadn't run into the sunset to be with the man of her dreams. She was sitting at her desk, writing about the love she'd lost. It was tragic and would be anything but a classic. I stopped writing and poured a glass of wine. It was needed.

It was December now. The holly bushes were covered in ice and fairy lights twinkled on houses. It was the most magical time of the year but for the first time in months I didn't feel merry. I felt kind of foolish actually. I'd been writing about the dream man, the man I'd fanaticised about but that man hadn't called in almost four months. I didn't know where he was and truth be told, he'd probably be wooing the next girl by now. Rose, you're an idiot.

I finished the bottle and snacked on the gingerbread that Susie had baked for me – well Eve had done so but Susie had helped lick the bowl. The next year was going to be the year I published a book, the year I made it. That dream was slowly slipping away. How would I finish it? I could make it up but it wouldn't have heart, it wouldn't be real. And then I'd spend my life answering whether the girl was me and I'd have to lie. I wasn't fabulous. I had run away from a chance at love, a shot at life. I felt like that thirty something spinster once more. I'd be just like Bridget Jones and too live a long and happy life with a bottle of wine. How depressing.

I spent the next few days wallowing in my own self pity. Eve called. She'd been mad at me for weeks after the whole Mark fiasco. She couldn't believe that I'd gone behind her back and dated him. She said it would have ended in tears and she was right. I'd fought back after all these years but he could have had his wicked way with me once again. And I had worn the dress. The black satin dress was one of Mark's favourites, the one I'd worn when he'd first seduced me. I was asking for it. I'd gone on that date wanting him. I'd apologised to Eve over and over. She said I didn't need to but I did. She'd defended me, comforted me time and time again and I still went back for more. Well, it was well and truly over now. It was the past.

'Hey you' I answered.

'Fancy a mulled wine at the markets tonight? Just us two' she said.

'Sounds perfect' I replied.

She met me at Covent Garden that evening. The lights twinkled in the square, the tree twice as big as the year before. We warmed up with a mulled wine. It was festivity in a mug.

'It gets better every year' I said, swirling around the orange and cinnamon.

'Doesn't it just?' she replied taking a gulp.

Eve loved the festive season. She craved the food, the cheer and the winter walks. She always had. And it was that little bit more magical with Susie. Susie's eyes lit up with the lights and Eve had even taken her to Santa's grotto this year. He'd asked her if she was on the nice list. Susie tugged his beard, grabbed her present and ran. She was a little diva at times.

'How's the book?' asked Eve. It was the dreaded question.

'Good' I replied.

It wasn't good at all. I'd written half a novel and now had writer's block.

'How are things with you?' I asked, changing the subject.

'I need a forty eight hour day' she said, rolling her eyes.

She spoke about how hard H was working at the office – late night meetings and weekend business calls. They hadn't had a night together for weeks. Susie had hit the terrible twos and was a bit of a handful. Every other word was *no*. She wanted chocolate for breakfast every morning and wouldn't brush her teeth before bed.

'I'm exhausted' sighed Eve.

And I thought I had problems. Love wasn't easy after all. We wandered around the market stalls, looking at glass decorations and knitted mittens. The food was something clsc. There were strawberries coated in chocolate, hog roast baps and every kind of cheese known to man. I sampled the cheeses, as always. I chose the stilton with pistachio and orange after much deliberation. We listened to the carols and spoke of our family plans over the holidays. Eve invited me for Christmas Eve drinks. It was something we did every year. She'd put Susie to bed, pop the presents under the tree and we'd drink Baileys over ice and watch *The Holiday*. H would munch his way through Santa's tray and re-fill the brandy glass a few dozen times. I did love this time of year. I just wish I too had a little family of my own to celebrate with.

'Have you heard anything from him?' Eve asked after one too many mulled wines.

She meant Onur. It was a touchy subject. She knew not to speak of him but we'd chat about him from time to time. I shook my head.

'I want to call him' I said softly.

'Why don't you then?' she asked.

I guess it was simple enough. I had his number and all I had to do was call.

'What would I say?' I asked, looking down.

I'd gone over this in my head a hundred times. What if he too dodged my calls? I couldn't bear the thought of it. He wasn't going to call any time soon. He thought it was over. I guess it was down to me.

'Hey' Eve said, lifting my chin. 'You're fabulous. He asked you to marry him for goodness sake. He loved you and I reckon he still does. Call him.'

We walked on. It was a mild winter's evening, the sky clear overhead. Eve was busy buying Susie a pink bobble hat – it was adorable – and I browsed the nearby stalls. There were boiled sweets, candy canes and Turkish delight. It was a sign. It was now or never. I dialled his number, my heart racing. It rang and rang and nothing. The line went dead. I tried a second time but still nothing. I stood there, numb. Had he screened the call? Perhaps he was busy? I didn't know what to think. I had broken his heart.

'What's wrong?' said Eve, turning around.

'He didn't answer' I replied, tears running down my face.

'Oh Rose.' She held me tightly and I sobbed. I'd made a mistake and it was too late to change it. I'd lost him forever.

Chapter Twenty Three

Plan *get my life back on track* took just over a week. I'd spent days sobbing over the dream man and hadn't written a word since. I'd eaten two jars of peanut butter and a dozen mince pies – even that hadn't helped. Eve had called every day, bless her. She said that I should take a leap of faith, fly out there and declare my love for him. It would certainly make a good ending to the story if nothing else. I'd considered it twice, more than that actually. She made it sound so easy, so romantic but the reality was a little different. What if there was someone else? What if he said no? Hugh had turned down Julia – that's just a film Rose. Everyone had told me to listen to my heart but my head was telling me otherwise.

It was two weeks until Christmas and the days flew by. I was living at the restaurant. Donatella told us time and time again that this was our busiest time. Fairy lights twinkled, everyone was cheery and tips were even better. There was a frost outside, the windows icy. I'd always loved this time of year. It was magical. Couples dined by candlelight, hand in hand and friends laughed over hearty Italian food. Antonio had baked Panettone and the smell of cinnamon lingered in the air.

'Any plans tonight?' he asked as we closed up.

He'd always stay and help me sweep the floor.

'I have a date with a bottle of wine' I replied.

He laughed.

'And you?' I asked.

He shook his head. '*Niente*' he said.

He'd wanted to ask me out for some time but never had – thank goodness. He was a sweetheart but I just didn't see him that way. There was no spark, no magic. He stayed a little longer and we chatted into the night. He was leaving for Italy tomorrow for the holidays.

'Merry Christmas Rose' he said warmly as he left.

'And to you' I beamed.

I walked home and the streets were still alive, even at this hour. There were market stalls and late night shopping. It was cold but laughter warmed the night. I did love it. I walked on and there was a wish tree – handwritten wishes for charity. I popped a few coins in the jar and read over the baubles. There were wishes for health, dreams for the future and hopes for joy. There was no mention of wealth or beauty. These were selfless wishes. I took off my mittens and wrote down a wish of my own. I kissed the paper ornament and walked on in the hope that it may come true. I guess you're never too old to believe in a little magic. Well, that's what my mother always said.

I did it. I can't believe I did it. What was I thinking? I'd drank a bottle – okay two bottles – of wine, watched *Love Actually* and had just done it. I had booked a one way ticket to be with the man of my dreams in a matter of days. And what's more, he didn't even know. The man I longed for had no idea that I'd be flying thousands of miles to declare my love for him. I'd listened to my heart, and Eve. It seemed like a great idea but now I wasn't so sure.

'You did it!' screamed Eve.

I'd called her that morning. I needed to tell someone.

'When do you leave?' she asked.

'Thursday' I replied.

'Christmas Eve?!' She shrieked.

'Yep' I answered. 'It's a bad idea isn't it?'

'No!' She yelled, waking Susie. She cursed under her breath and lowered her voice. 'You need to do this, you need to know. It's now or never. And if it doesn't go to plan then get a fabulous tan, come back for New Year's Eve and we'll get sloshed on bubbly.'

She was right. I needed to know if I still had a shot at love. It was now or never. He could say yes and we'd live happily ever after. If not, then I'd write this year off as the biggest mistake of my life, drown my sorrows and begin the next decade with half a dozen resolutions. It was the perfect plan.

'Come help me pack?' I asked.

'I wouldn't miss it for the world' she replied.

I had butterflies and it was like prom night all over again. I didn't even know if he'd be there. I didn't have a clue where he'd be in the city so I'd booked a flight to his hometown. I'd go to his house and that was really the end of my plan. I'd work it out somehow. The truth being, it wasn't just Onur I wanted. I'd missed the dreamy life. Perhaps I'd stay even if he said no. It would be like Shirley Valentine where she falls in love with her life once more. And that's what I needed to do, to live again.

'You're leaving?' shouted Donatella.

I nodded, handing her my notice. Well, it wasn't much of a notice in truth. I'd told her I'd be happy to work the next day or so but that would be all and I wasn't sure when I'd come back, if ever.

'Very well' she said, pursing her lips.

I couldn't help but smile. She thought I'd be there for some time, years perhaps.

'Thank you for everything' I said and I meant it.

'You'll be back' she snapped and turned on her heel.

'Not this time' I whispered under my breath.

I hadn't told my parents. Dad knew nothing of Onur and how could I tell Mum that I was leaving. They'd be crushed that I wouldn't be here for Christmas. It would be our first one apart.

'I'm leaving to go and be with the man I love' I said in the mirror over and over.

I cringed each and every time. Maybe I should just leave a note, better still a post-it. I could say I was going away with Ivy? She'd be with Ted. Why didn't I have any single girlfriends? That was a depressing thought.

'I'm leaving to go and-'

'Be with the man you love' said Mum, sadness in her voice.

I turned around and we looked at each other for some time.

'Go sweetheart' she said, tears running down her face.

I held her tightly. We both knew that one day we'd have to say goodbye. This wasn't goodbye but it was for now.

'You shall go to the ball' she said as she had done when I was little. And just like that, Cinderella was on her way to find her prince.

We sat on the floor and chatted through the night. She'd made hot chocolate – with cream and a shot of Baileys of course – and I told her all. I spoke of the romance, the butterflies. She smiled and said that's how she'd felt when she met Dad and still did.

'You just know' she said.

'Can you tell him?' I asked.

I was still his little girl and he'd only worry. She nodded.

It was the perfect winter evening and one I'd remember for a long time. I'd miss them, of course I would but everyone has their lives to live and it was time for me to live mine.

It was soon the day before the big day. Eve was at mine for eleven, armed with champagne and tissues.

'Isn't it a little early?' I asked opening the door, still in my pyjamas.

'It's never too early for champagne' she said and winked.

I opened the case. This was going to be tricky. I brushed my hand across the rail of clothes. Eve had final say of whether I take it, throw it or leave it – very *Sex and the City*. She vetoed most of the dresses.

'You don't need that' she said.

This was harder than I thought but I guess she was right. Life was simpler in the sunshine. Onur was a humble man and what's more, he didn't have a Prada shirt to match the Versace dress anyway. It took four hours to fit twenty four years into one suitcase. I'd packed the Manolos – I needed them to take me home – and a little of everything else. I was ready. Eve and I drank the rest of bubbly and reminisced.

'I still can't believe you're going Ro' she said.

'It feels like a dream' I replied.

'Here's to your happily ever after' she said, raising her glass to mine.

'Let's hope so' I said.

Eve stayed until later that evening. We laughed about our high school crushes, our prom dresses and all of the wonderful memories we shared along the way. She'd always been there for me and I hoped we'd always be close. Who knew where life would take us.

'I'm jealous' she said.

'You're jealous of me?' I laughed.

I'd always been a little jealous of Eve and her perfect life.

'I am' she answered. 'It's an adventure, the unknown. And I'll be here, changing nappies.'

'The unknown can be enchanting' Mustafa had said all those months ago and it was true.

Eve had to go to put Susie to bed not long after. She'd been a nightmare at bath time and H was having a meltdown.

'Go and live your best life' Eve said, tearing up.

'Give Susie a kiss from me' I replied.

We held each other and I blew her a kiss as she left, with a handful of my clothes I might add.

It was surreal. I looked around my room, at the packed suitcase in the corner. I could remember packing all those months ago, not knowing where life would take me but this time I knew.

The flight was at ten the next morning. Mum had told Dad a white lie for now – I was visiting a friend I'd met over there for the holidays. She said she'd tell him the truth later but I think he knew deep down. The roads were quiet.

Everyone was with their families, drinking mulled wine and eating all things sweet. I'd miss it but there was always next year. Dad helped me with my case – it wasn't as heavy as last time – and they walked me to the check-in desks. This was it, this was goodbye.

'Take care sweetheart' cried Mum.

'Be safe titch' Dad said softly.

I didn't know when I'd see them again and that really hit home.

'I love you to the top of the Eiffel Tower and back' she whispered in my ear and kissed me tenderly.

I watched them walk away, hand in hand. I blew them a kiss and wiped away the tears. They'd always be my home.

This was it. I was all set. I'd checked in, made my way through security and treated myself to a little Jo Malone in duty free. It was red roses – very apt. I browsed the shops but didn't need anything. I'd spent years filling a void with pretty things. I only needed one thing now and that was him – the blue-eyed boy. It wasn't long before the flight was called. It all felt like a bit of a blur. I was daydreaming and it was like a dream. I took my seat and gazed out of the window. It was a crisp winter's day and the sun broke through the clouds.

'Hello pet!'

You have to be kidding me. I'd recognise her anywhere. She was dressed head to toe in leopard print, her blonde curls permed.

'Hi Cathy' I replied.

'Looks like I'm sat behind you dear' she chuckled, squeezing into her seat. She was jolly, even more so than before.

The stewardess came down the aisle with refreshments not long after take-off. I'd promised Eve I'd get a bottle of champagne to toast the new life.

'Champagne please' I said. 'And two glasses' I added, winking at Cathy.

I told her all about the dream man and she raised her plastic flute to mine. Everyone was listening and I didn't care. I was living life the way I wanted to. The couple next to me raised their brows, judging me of course.

'I wish I'd done the same pet. Live while you're young' Cathy said, hiccupping on the fizz.

'Here's to living' I said and took a gulp.

Cathy dozed off mid flight, tipsy on the bubbles. We were somewhere over The Mediterranean and we bobbed above the clouds. I had something to write about. There was more than just the ordinary. I was living. I jotted down my thoughts on the back of *Vogue* – sacrilege I know.

'I'll meet you across the seas my love as no distance could ever be too far.'

I fastened my seatbelt as we prepared for landing. Cathy handed me a boiled sweet. She'd not long been awake. I'd slept a little myself – it was that third glass of bubbly. I looked out of the window. This was it, the start of my new life. It was mid afternoon, the sky a brilliant blue. The mountains were coated with snow in the distance, dreamy nonetheless. The plane jolted, hitting the runway with a thud. And I was home.

'That fizz has gone right to my head' Cathy chuckled.

She rummaged in the overhead locker for her leopard print case. There was too much print – a fashion nightmare. We walked through the terminal, chatting away. She really was a breath of fresh air.

'Good luck sweetheart' she said as we parted ways.

I couldn't help but smile as she tottered off with her bags. I doubt I'd sec her again but she'd live a merry life. I was sure of that.

I took a taxi down to the town and it was just how I'd rcmembered. It was still warm, even in the winter months. Locals drank coffee on the harbour, the fishing boats bobbing away on the waves. The sun was lower, the sky a shade of pink. Couples strolled hand in hand in the early evening. Life was peaceful. It was always summer here. There were no gingerbread houses, twinkling lights or overpriced hot chocolates. Life was bright and as magical as I'd dreamed. This is where I belonged.

I'd asked the driver to drop me by the harbour. He'd taken the scenic route, circling the waterfront at least twice. I didn't mind. I'd never grow tired of seeing this place. I'd booked a hotel, just in case, but first I needed to clear my head. I couldn't face it all, not just yet. I walked along the cobbles to a bench, our bench. That was a lifetime ago and the blossom was no longer in flower. It was a little like our love but there was hope that too would bloom once more. I sat and looked out to sea. The water moved gently, the sun setting. It was quiet. I inhaled the sea air and the sky became an orange hue.

What would I say to him? Would he even be there? The sky darkened and I felt foolish. I shouldn't go. I'd get that fabulous tan, drink a little wine and go home, back to reality. And then it hit me. This wasn't just about him. I was where I'd dreamed of being for months, perhaps even years. Why should I throw it all away? I wanted a shot at love but maybe I could still have the happily ever after. I sat there a little longer. It was getting late and cooler still. I'd asked for a taxi at the restaurant. It was the place we'd had our moonlight date, our last night together. It was bitter sweet – more sweet than bitter but still. Oh how I longed for him. Would it be too late?

'Taxi' said the waiter. He helped me with my bags and was happy to do so.

The driver drove on past the harbour. It was dark now, the street lights lighting the paths. It was only a matter of minutes before he stopped. I stepped out of the taxi, the saltiness of the water still in the air. He heaved the case out of the trunk and I walked inside. It was a stone building covered with what would be blossom in the spring. The receptionist welcomed me and handed over the keys. I procrastinated a little, stalling. Come on Rose, you can do this. And with that, I dumped the case in the room and misted my skin with red roses. I closed my eyes and pictured the rose he'd once given to me. I couldn't help but smile and then I was on my way.

It wasn't far. I walked down the dusty alleyways, a right turn and then left again. The dim street lights lit the way. I'd seen this street in my dreams a hundred times over. There were no crickets now, no summer breeze. I stood in front of the white washed house, the paint still cracked. I saw it for what it was. It was a home, a home filled with love. I took a deep breath and knocked. There was no answer. I knocked again. The outside light flickered and the door opened ever so slightly. I felt nauseous, my heart racing. This was it.

The door opened a little more. It was his mother. She looked frail, not quite as I'd remembered. I smiled but her face was blank. Did she remember me? She stared at me, her lips pursed. I drew breath to speak but she shook her head, waving her arms and slammed the door. I stood there for a moment. It was over. There was no hope.

Chapter Twenty Four

We were over. I'd been kidding myself the whole time. I'd broken his heart, dodged his calls and still expected him to be waiting with open arms. How foolish. Even his mother hated me. I couldn't help but wonder what he'd told them. I glanced up to the stars, holding back the tears and dreamed to be dancing underneath them, even if it was just one last time. There wouldn't be another date. It was over. I turned and walked back down the street. It was even cooler now. I felt nothing. It wasn't just Onur but he was a big part of the life I dreamed of. I'd let him slip through my fingers and I hated myself for not believing in our love. I'd made a mistake and now it was too late. I stilled, hearing footsteps behind me. I turned around. There was someone in the shadows. And then she came closer.

'Ela?'

She was just as I'd remembered – her brown locks bouncing, her skin flawless. She looked sad, no longer lighting the room as she had once done.

'Rose' she began.

I was unsure of what she'd say. I half expected the street to chase me with pitchforks at this point.

'I'm sorry about that' she said, gesturing towards the house.

'I understand' I replied softly.

'Things are complicated at the minute' she said, tears in her eyes.

'Are you okay?' I asked. She didn't look it.

'Not really' she said. 'Onur wasn't the same once you left and...' she took a deep breath '...our father died.'

The words hit me. Their father had passed away. I couldn't begin to imagine what they were going through.

'Ela, I'm so sorry' I said, holding her. She poured her heart out, sobbing. It was still raw. 'When did this happen?'

'Four months ago' she sniffled.

Four months? That was when I'd left. The night I'd flown home. That would have been the night he called. Tears gathered in my eyes. He'd tried to reach out to me and I'd done nothing. His father was the glue that held them all together and now he was gone. I didn't know what to say. I just held her.

Time passed and nothing was said. She was lifeless, like a rag doll. I wondered how she'd ever get over it. She was only in her twenties, in her prime of life. He'd never be able to give her away on her wedding day or see his grandchildren grow. I couldn't picture life without my father and I wouldn't want to. How had he died? He wasn't old, he looked well. There were questions to be asked but now wasn't the time. We sat on the wall outside her home. It was cold but neither of us noticed. I wiped the tears from her face as she pulled away.

'Ela, where is Onur?' I asked softly, hope in my voice.

I needed to know, now more than ever. Life really is too short. She looked down, unsure of whether to say.

'Please' I begged.

She bit her lip. 'He's here' she said.

I wasn't expecting it. I was speechless. I looked at the house. He was here. The man I longed for was so close, yet so far. I didn't know what to do.

'He's not at home' she then said.

She went on to tell me that he was working in a bar along the harbour. It turns out that he'd never gone back to the city. He was the man of the house now. That was him all over. He'd sacrificed his own dreams for his family. I didn't think I could love the man anymore but I was wrong. Perhaps he'd moved on, perhaps he never wanted to see me again but I had to find out. Ela jotted down the name of the place and wished me luck. I gave her another squeeze and thanked her. I could have walked away and he'd have never even known I'd been here.

I rushed to the harbour. I was out of breath and covered in dust from the lanes. I walked along the cobbled path in search of the place. I could think nothing other than seeing him. I didn't care how I looked – there was a first for everything – or if I made a fool of myself. I stood in front of the building for a moment, not knowing what to do. This was it. I took a deep breath and walked inside. It was an old building with wooden decking, cushioned seating and fairy lights. I couldn't see him. I was desperate, craving him once more. I spun around and stilled. There he was. He was standing behind the bar. He wore a shirt, partly unbuttoned and rolled up at the sleeve. He looked better than I'd dreamed. I was taken back to the magic, to the hope of love. And then he looked up. He stared at me as he had done so in the very beginning. He wasn't smug this time, his face was blank. I lost track of how long we stood there, just staring at one another. Neither one of us moved. I was here to declare my love for him and I only hoped he felt the same. And just like that he jumped over the wood and ran towards me. He lifted me high into the air and kissed me. It was love at first sight.

'*Gülüm*' he whispered in my ear. And I was his.

Everyone applauded. The lights twinkled and I was high on love once more. It was the romantic ending I'd been searching for. Onur shouted something to the guy behind the bar and he nodded, tossing him his jacket.

'Shall we?' he said, gesturing towards the door.

We walked in silence. There were things to be said but none of it now mattered. He loved me. He'd never stopped loving me. And I loved him, more so than I'd ever imagined. The sky was dark, the moon lighting the way. We strolled side by side and came to our bench. It was where we'd sat all those months ago, where I'd since sat wondering what may be.

'Rose' he said. Oh how he curled his tongue around my name.

I gazed into those blue irises, brighter than ever. He pulled me close and kissed my forehead. He smelt the same – cigarettes and aftershave. He said nothing else and we sat there for some time beneath the blanket of stars.

How could I explain it? I'd broken this heart yet he loved me still. He had nothing to say and why would he? It was all me. It had been my doing.

'I'm sorry' I said softly.

He lifted my chin, his touch warming. 'You came back' he said, smiling.

'I promised' I replied.

'Why did you come?' he asked.

'I love you' I said, tears in my eyes. It was the truth.

He smirked a little. He said nothing but pulled something from his pocket. His grandmother's ring, the one he'd once given to me. He'd carried it around this whole time in the hope I'd come back to him. The diamonds twinkled under the streetlight.

'I hoped' he said, shrugging.

I held out my hand and he slipped the ring onto my finger where it belonged.

'Father told me to give it to you. Life is too short' he said.

He was right. Not one of us knew how long we'd be here for but by god I knew how I wanted to live. I wanted to spend the days under the sun, the nights dancing beneath the stars. I wanted the romance, the love, the happily ever after. I now knew that it was real. True love does last a lifetime and I'd finally found the one I wanted to spend mine with.

'Wishes do come true' he said.

He spoke of the dandelion wish. The wish he'd never told. He'd wished for me, for my love and I had the love story I'd wished for. In every corner of the world, there is a love story waiting to be told, you just have to find it. And just like that, I believed in magic.

Chapter Twenty Five

One Year Later

Onur had been up all night working on his paper. He'd taken a year out from his studies but he'd never given up on his dreams. The professor said he could finish his degree when the time was right. Now was that time. He had spent the past year working day and night, saving every penny. It was all for us. He was driven to better himself, to give us a better life. I couldn't be more proud. He may not have millions but I didn't care. Nothing mattered, apart from the love we had. He looked peaceful as he slept.

It was mid morning. I made my way to the kitchen, pouring a cup of coffee. I was still in my nightie but time didn't matter. I stood by the open window and looked out to the world for some time. The smell of mint rose from the garden. Orange trees lined the house and birds perched on the windowsill. It was quiet, the air fresh. This is how I'd spend my mornings. There was no rush, no plan. I'd water the rose bushes and trim a single bud, placing it in a vase on the breakfast table. I'd pick oranges from the tree and pop the freshly laid eggs – yes we have chickens – in a basket. Life was wonderful. I hadn't yet been back to London and I didn't miss it in the slightest. There was an odd time when I fancied a toasted crumpet or that peanut butter fix but I soon got over it. Eve called every week to chat – oh how I missed her – and Susie loved our calls. She was growing fast and her personality was more adorable now than ever.

'Auntie Rosie, I'm a princess' she said just last week.

She was obsessed with princesses and fairy tales, just like I had been when I was her age. Eve told me that she'd watch Cinderella at least twice a day and hum the songs, waving her magic wand. I'd love to give her chocolate kisses again but now I sent stardust overseas and that was even better.

Eve told me a few weeks back that there was trouble in paradise. She was talking about Mark. H had told her that he'd blown most of his inheritance – just shy of two million – on women, holiday homes and fancy dinner dates. I wanted to feel sorry for the guy but I couldn't. He was single and broke. Money was all that he'd had and now he'd have to earn it. There would be no more oysters or caviar now and he'd be anything but smug.

I strolled down the garden path to the bench, shaded beneath the trees. It was a little like our bench, the blossom covered one along the harbour. I loved to sit here. The garden was pretty and I had Dad to thank for that. They'd visited a few months back and had fallen in love with the place I now call home. Dad planted herbs and pruned the roses whilst Mum and I drank cosmopolitans on the porch. It was then that Mum had given me her gold locket. She'd had it since I was little. It had a photo of me inside, my teeth marks etched into the gold. It was priceless. I opened the pendant to find a photo of my parents and from that very day I'd never taken it off. They may not be here but they'd always be close to my heart. I smiled as I thought of them.

I'd sit here and read many a day. I'd even got Onur to read a couple of classics and he'd loved them. The house was filled with oak furniture. I adored the desk which we'd stumbled across in an antique store. It now held photos of our life together, including our first photo together. That felt like a lifetime ago but it always made me smile. My favourite piece stood in the hallway, pride of place. We'd found a carpenter in the town who was more than happy to custom build the bookcase I'd dreamed of. It was filled with all of the love stories I adored. The wood was twisted and dark and had character like no other. And there it was, on the centre shelf. *In Any Language, It's You I love* – the tale of love across two countries. I'd finished our love story and the publishers jumped at the idea. I was an author. The sales hadn't been huge – well not yet anyway – but that didn't matter. I'd done what I'd always dreamed and couldn't be happier. I'd spend my days writing, reading and whatever else took my fancy. Just last week I'd joined a pottery class and dabbled in a little painting. The world really is my oyster.

Onur's mother had taught me to cook some traditional Turkish dishes – stuffed aubergines, hummus and minted yoghurt amongst a few. She'd bring terracotta pots filled with spices, herbs and fresh vegetables to our home. She'd chat away and we'd drink tea in the garden. She loved having us close by. I found that I could understand more each day. It only took a little practice.

Ela had been working as model for Turkish *Vogue* – yes *Vogue*! It didn't surprise me really, she was a natural beauty. She'd been obsessed ever since I left her the glossy magazine. She lived in the city but always visited with the goods she'd been given. There was a little Chanel here and Prada there. I'd spend hours talking couture with her over the champagne she'd bring. It was the little bit of luxury that I did miss from time to time. And I now read *Vogue* but in a different language and loved it all the same.

Onur stood by the door. He was as handsome as ever, shirtless with bed hair.

'Good morning my dear wife' he said softly.

That's right, we were married. He didn't want me making a run for it once again so he said we should just do it and I couldn't think why not. We were wed in the spring, beneath the stars. I'd worn my mother's dress – ivory slow satin – and carried a dozen red roses. Onur wore a black tuxedo and looked dapper as always. It was a small ceremony. There were only a handful of guests, those closest to our hearts. Eve was maid of honour and wore a champagne gown and Susie was flower girl in the cutest of dresses. She skipped down the aisle, humming and throwing rose petals. Elvis' *'Can't Help Falling in Love'* serenaded all as we danced as husband and wife. Everyone was high on cake, bubbly and love. And he was stuck with me until death do us part. It wasn't the big wedding I thought we'd have, it was better. We'd bought our home instead of splurging on a big day – well three days. It didn't matter, what mattered was that we were together. And with each day that passed I loved him more.

'Good morning my husband' I replied.

I still couldn't quite get used to it. I was married. I'd found my Prince Charming and life was just how I'd always imagined. He stared at me for some time, as he always did. I read the pages of *Love Letters of Great Men*, happy that I'd too found love. I should really get started on the next book. The publishers were eager to know what happened next in the love story but I didn't know what tomorrow would bring and that was the best part. Onur sat beside me, his arm around me. This is where I was happiest, in his arms. He read the morning paper and ate a little fresh bread. I even baked now too. I found I had the time to do whatever I wanted.

'How is she?' he asked.

'She's perfect' I said.

He kissed my forehead and then kissed bump. It had come as a little surprise but I was so in love already – a little love to warm our hearts. She would be a mini me, a mini English Rose. It was everything I'd wished for and more. It was the happy ever after, the fairy tale.

Printed in Great Britain
by Amazon

44106992R00151